# the ART of
# FRENCH
# ~~COOKING~~
# KISSING

Also by Brianna R. Shrum
*Never Never*
*How to Make Out*

# the ART OF
# FRENCH
# ~~COOKING~~
# KISSING

## Brianna R. Shrum

Sky Pony Press
New York

Sky Pony Press books may be purchased in bulk at special discounts for sales promotion, corporate gifts, fund-raising, or educational purposes. Special editions can also be created to specifications. For details, contact the Special Sales Department, Sky Pony Press, 307 West 36th Street, 11th Floor, New York, NY 10018 or info@skyhorsepublishing.com.

Sky Pony® is a registered trademark of Skyhorse Publishing, Inc.®, a Delaware corporation.

Visit our website at www.skyponypress.com.

10 9 8 7 6 5 4 3 2 1

Library of Congress Cataloging-in-Publication Data is available on file.

Cover design by Kate Gartner

Print ISBN: 978-1-5107-3205-6
Ebook ISBN: 978-1-5107-3206-3

Printed in the United States of America

*For Harry,*

*Kicking my butt at grilled cheese since junior year <3*

# CHAPTER ONE

There is a very particular art to the making of grilled cheese. To making the *perfect* grilled cheese, at least. It's so much more than just slapping a slice of Velveeta between some white bread and letting the thing languish in a skillet. A grilled cheese, when done right, with melty strings of provolone and buttered French bread crisped to golden brown, is a culinary wonder.

My essay written to perfection on grilled cheese is going to get me into the Savannah Institute of Culinary Arts. Or at least, into their scholarship competition.

I reread it before I touch the envelope staring up at me on my bed. It's good. It's simple, so no one will have thought to write about it twelve weeks ago, and I can just about taste the butter and cheese wafting out of my computer screen. Or I could when I wrote it. Right now, the only flavor I detect is the very distinct old acetone on my fingernails and who knows what under them. Possibly some sweat drifting down from my upper lip. Anxiety is about to eat me alive.

*Open it. Open the thing. It is a prewritten piece of paper; it cannot hurt you.*

Sticks and stones, man. *But words of rejection from the only school in the world that matters can ALWAYS hurt me.*

I slam my hands down onto my ratty mattress and the envelope doesn't move. Because it is heavy—heavy with secrets.

I read the address typed in a neat sans serif in the top left-hand corner again and again, and then my own name in the middle. I have to look. If I'm in, I have to be ready to jet off to Savannah, Georgia, in three weeks.

I have to look because I need to know if it's time to drain half a semester's worth of after-school shifts waiting tables at Ryan's BBQ on a plane ticket. Plus, it'll take me the full three weeks to re-memorize every cookbook in the pantry and binge the last few seasons of *Top Chef* and do laundry. Clothes are important.

I grab my phone.

> **Carter:** HELPPPPPPPP MEEEEEEEEE
> **Em:** what do you need
> **Carter:** MAKE ME DO THE THING.
> **Em:** do the damn thing
> **Carter:** I CAN'T DO THE THING
> **Em:** good lord. do it. i am too tired for
>      this.

I raise my eyes to the sky and grab the envelope with shaking fingers. This is it. In or out.

And I rip.

It takes me a good thirty seconds to pull the paper out of the envelope, and another thirty to unfold it, but I do. And I force myself to look.

*Dear Ms. Lane,*
*We are pleased to extend to you an invitation to attend—*
My happy scream shakes the house.

"Are you dead?"

"Yes," I say. "And it's exactly how I would have chosen to die."

Em raises her bright red eyebrows and leans back against my wall. "Thought you always said your ideal was being kissed to death by Tom Hiddleston in a Loki outfit."

The corner of my mouth turns up. "Okay. This is the second way I would have chosen to die."

Em laughs. She has kind of a smoker's laugh. Em is particularly small, and her strawberry blonde hair is particularly large, and she looks like a little thing you would find flitting from flower to flower in Thumbelina's army, but when she speaks, her voice is throaty, raspy, almost as low as a boy's. And she holds herself in a way that makes people leap out of her path. We've been friends since the third grade, and she's always been that way. I am the purple-haired Marcie to her Peppermint Patty, I think.

Em says, "So you're abandoning me for the coast all summer then."

I groan and she smiles.

"I'm messing with you," she says. "You should go, of course, and I'll just waste away by the city pool all break."

"Please," I say. "If by 'waste away,' you mean 'finally get into Sophie Travers's *Baywatch*-red swimsuit while on-duty' then yes. You will waste away at the city pool."

"Excuse you; lifeguarding is about saving *lives*."

"Yeah," I say, eyes narrow.

Em flips me off but smirks, whorls of hair spreading out all over my wall. "I would die to get into Sophie Travers's swimsuit. Ugh. You perv. *Get into her swimsuit*."

"You like it."

"I do."

I can't let go of the acceptance letter so it's just sitting there, crinkling in my hand. I'm probably sweating all over it in excited anxiety, words so blurry Mom and Dad won't even be able to read it when they get home. Man. I don't even know why this is such a massive deal; it's a competition. Not a guarantee. In fact, it's way less than a guarantee—it's a cutthroat war between like a billion of the top high school culinary students in the country. All competing for one scholarship. One scholarship to *the* school. The top three runners up get a little but it's jack compared to full ride. Room and board, everything.

It's a freaking dream, and I don't know how to manage my feelings.

"Carter," Em says sharply, whacking me on the forehead.

"Yeah? Yeah, sorry. I was . . . can you say that again?"

Em narrows her eyes and says, very slowly, "Sophie is coming over to my place next weekend. Sophie. Of the *Baywatch*-red swimsuit. To my place. To like, study, but I'm hoping also to not. I don't know. But she's gonna be there until whenever. While Mom is working late."

"For real?" I say.

"Thank you; that is the reaction I was looking for."

"Sorry," I say, and I hold out the invitation. "I'm just—I can't even process this. This is what I've wanted since I was fourteen. This school. This program. If I get that scholarship, it's like, like I could actually *go* . . ." I let my head drop into my hands, because sometimes excitement feels like terror.

This cocktail is all of that plus the awesome bonus of: if I lose, I will have lost half-to-a-whole summer I could have been working, plus all that airfare, and then how will I pay for school books? And more college apps? And all these things I could have cobbled together on tuition that my parents sure as *hell* can't pay for.

It's fine.

Everything is fine.

"You're gonna get it," she says, resting her hand on mine. "I know it." I hear the laugh in her voice when she adds, "With grilled cheeses like yours, how could you fail?"

I say into my hands, "It sounded like you said, 'Grilled Jesus.'"

"Don't get cocky. Your food is good but not worthy of a world religion."

I snort and stand. "Come downstairs. I'll make you some food to worship."

Em grabs my hand, and whenever she does this, I am struck by the sheer number of freckles on her skin. She has so many, I sometimes wonder how they can all fit on her tiny body.

When we walk into the kitchen, my older sister, Jillian, is there eating a bowl of cereal, and Mom and Dad come bustling in.

"Did you find out yet?" is the first thing my mom says, and I take a deep breath, running my hand through my hair. I'll have to re-dye before I go; the purple is fading out of the ends.

"Yeah," I say.

My dad walks up behind her, hands on her shoulders, as if this is a big event in Mom's life or something. And their faces are so wild-eyed, so hopeful, that I start laughing, and then they know. They know I made it.

"Yeahhhhh, Carter!" Jillian says, milk sloshing over the edge of her bowl and onto me, and she throws the spoon-holding arm around my neck. My parents join and that's kind of embarrassing, honestly—the 1950s family overcuteness in front of Em. But Em has been in and out of here for a million years, and she is used to it, I'm certain. It's the opposite of her house—hers is quiet all the time, just her and her neurosurgeon mom, whereas here, it's basically constant activity and balloons and shouting every time someone comes home with an A on an exam.

"Please try not to cry when you realize you will be deprived of my presence for the duration of the summer," I say. "Or do cry. But do it when I have to spy on you to witness."

"Scout's honor," says Dad.

I push past everyone to sweep an entire loaf of sliced French bread into a pan. Cooking usually falls to me. Which is the way I like it.

Everyone just naturally settles at the table, which has one leg shorter than the others, its stain rubbing off it more and more every year. I pull out this old, crooked sauté pan and heat it.

6

I wonder if all the equipment there will be state-of-the-art. If all the other kids will have learned to cook from real classes in amazing kitchens, if they'll all know what they're doing.

I wonder, now that it's here in my reach, if I have any real business going there or if I'm just good at writing poetry about grilled cheese.

Because wanting something like this? Dreaming about it? When all these other contestants are probably legit and I'm. Well. Someone like me. Is *terrifying*.

I shut my eyes and smell the butter. Shut out all this anxiety that wants to drown me. Focus on the scent and the sizzle and let myself fall into the food and the movement of this old-as-hell pan.

I breathe.

"Thank you," I whisper to the bread in one of my hands and the provolone in the other. "You got this for me. Now we just have to win it."

# CHAPTER TWO

The first thing I learn when I set foot on SICU's campus is that I am woefully unprepared for this. The second is that I hate Reid Yamada. Both of these things reveal themselves in a single incident.

I drag my suitcase (which is a rolling BB-8; I make no apologies) up the little sidewalk that twists and turns its way up to the school, bumping over every square of pavement. I feel like I'm swimming just walking through the air here, like I am suspended in one giant raindrop, and by the time I finally reach the massive double doors of the school, I am drenched. It's not raining, so I don't even really want to think about the implications of that beyond the fact that I am vaguely disgusting, and this college looks like something out of *The Hunchback of Notre Dame*: bright green everywhere on the grounds, and brick and spires that jut up from the earth to make me extremely, positively certain that I am not worthy.

I push through the doors, half wondering if I'll discover that the staircases move and I'm late for the Sorting Ceremony when I step inside. I am only slightly disappointed when I find neither of those things, instead ending up somewhere I think I want to stay forever. The foyer is small from side to side but feels gigantic because of the ceiling. Golds and browns and reds everywhere, ornate rugs. . . . This looks like a place a ghost from the 1800s would haunt just to feel at home.

"Drop your things here," says someone to my left—brisk voice, sharp. I drop BB-8 immediately, then have to snatch him back up. She didn't literally mean "here" unless she wanted a giant pile of bags blocking the entry.

"Sorry," I say, managing to maneuver my rolly bag so deftly that it rolls right over the woman's foot not once, but twice. By the time I wrangle it into the side room, she has a perma-scowl on her face and she is peering into mine like she is going to systematically memorize and then destroy it.

"The students are gathering in the common room," she says, then she turns and slightly limps away.

I head forward past the stairs I presume leads to the dorms and follow the murmurs and shuffling, which get louder the farther I go. And then there they are—my competition. There are twenty-four of us, and it looks like I'm one of the last to arrive. Everyone is just kind of sitting on these little couches, talking or fidgeting, and it feels so big. We're in this small annex, and I know there are only a few dorms in here—it's the original building, the one they used when the school was tiny, before they had any idea what it would turn into, but it still . . . well . . . it feels like something major.

And maybe it is. This school has one of the highest job placements of any culinary school in the country after graduation. If I win, I could *do this thing*. I make my way forward and find an old, flowery-patterned couch with an empty cushion and sit.

"Hi," says the guy next to me, and I turn.

"Hi," I say, blinking stupidly for a second. Boys with smirking mouths and dark brown eyes are my kryptonite. And his black undercut is exceptionally, *exquisitely* floppy.

"Reid Yamada," he says, and he sticks out his hand. His fingers are long and slim—a pianist's hands.

I shake it, and say, "Carter."

He raises an eyebrow. "Carter . . .?"

"Sorry. Lane. Carter Lane." I am so stupid.

Reid nods and throws his arm over the back of the couch opposite of where I'm sitting. He leans back and smiles at me like this is nothing. Like he's just so relaxed. I, on the other hand, am wound so tight that I can do nothing but scrunch. My skin is scrunched, my muscles are scrunched, my bones are scrunched; I am an ode to the nineties hair accessory. And my thoughts are just scrambling over one another, each one terrorizing the next to get to the forefront of my brain. The only things that are even close to winning are "Hogwarts" and Reid's dark brown eyes, and so apparently I just say, "Harry Potter."

Reid raises an eyebrow. "I'm sorry?"

I am blushing. In addition to scrunching, now my skin and muscles and bones are all blushing. Furiously. "It just looks like it in here. I thought we'd walk in and get sorted first thing." I laugh, because I talk and laugh when I'm nervous. I'm a damn hyena. "Ten points to Ravenclaw," I say weakly in a horrific fake British accent.

Reid cocks his head, corner of his mouth turned up, and points to his chest. "Slytherin," he says.

"Of course." I wiggle my butt backward, trying to find a comfortable place on this couch, knocking into him a little, but he doesn't say anything. And the quiet is almost more unnerving than the talking. We're all just waiting here and I cannot stand it.

"So where are you from?" I say.

Reid's mouth draws in a bit, and he says, "Denver," then waits in what feels like a slightly defensive silence for a second before he says, "You?"

I furrow my brow but choose to ignore it. "Montana. Small town."

His face relaxes again. "Ah, then you have an advantage over me. Little towns like Savannah aren't gonna make you claustrophobic."

"Yeah," I say, smiling. "I'm your biggest competition."

That eyebrow quirks one more time, little smile on his lips. "You think?" he says, and something about the way he looks at me makes me flush all over. Again.

I open my mouth to respond but clap it closed like a trout because someone in very fancy slacks begins to speak in the front of the room.

"Welcome, SICU Scholarship Competitors!" she says. Her hair is pulled back into a severe-looking bun, drawing her pale skin back with it. But her eyes are bright and kind.

A few claps, and someone whoops in the background.

"As you know, the weeks—or days—you will spend here will be grueling. Brutal, cutthroat competition, though murder of your competitors is strictly forbidden."

I let out a little laugh, along with a few of the others, but Reid doesn't even crack a smile. He's completely zoned in, focused. I look back to the woman at the front.

"I am Dr. Lavell, head of this program. Tonight, you will meet several of my assistants, all professors on campus of one culinary specialty or another. They will be your judges for the remainder of the program. You will face a great number of challenges here, both individual and team-based—two per week, to be precise—and at the end of this week, three of you will be going home."

I swallow through the swift knot in my throat. And I am positive that the sudden wetness around my collar has nothing to do with the humidity.

"You will be divided into two arbitrary teams for the first part of the competition, where you will be judged as a team and on your ability to work cooperatively in a kitchen. There will be an individual component to judging, as well, which will contribute to the decisions regarding who stays and who goes."

I've been picking at the fabric of the couch I'm sitting on, and you can definitely see where it's frayed now. But it was an unconscious thing. I can't have been the first to nervously deface this property. I make myself breathe.

Wanting something this badly this early is so dangerous. Wanting something this badly at *all* is dangerous. It's what gets people totally trashed drunk, jumping in the pool fully clothed on night one of *The Bachelor* every year. They can't hack it. And if you can't stand the heat—no. I can't make a joke that corny, even in my own head.

"Now," says Dr. Lavell, "your room assignments will be posted just up the stairs. Boys' rooms on the right, girls' on the left, and—do not get up yet." Who here has a death wish? I tense up just from secondhand embarrassment. "I know you're all tired from traveling, but that doesn't make much difference here. Before you may go to your rooms, you all need to file out from this building to the large one across campus. Follow signs for the kitchen. Your first challenge awaits."

Panic wells in my chest when she turns on her heel and leaves the building, and students scramble up all at once to get to the kitchens. I'd counted on a night of sleep, a few hours of studying, something to wash away the plane grossness on my skin and the jet lag in my bones. Nope. We are being Gordon Ramsayed.

I jump up with everyone, trailing just behind Reid, who is no more than six inches taller than me, but his legs move like he's got a foot on me, minimum. I'm huffing and puffing already. Good lord.

"You coming?" he says over his shoulder, and I know he's talking to me.

There's a laugh in his voice, and a growl in mine when I say, "It's not a race; it's a *cooking competition*."

"Suit yourself," he says. "If my biggest competition is the one showing up last to every challenge, this should be an excellent summer."

He moves up ahead and I clench my jaw, head down against the wind. I will not be last.

I am last.

This humidity, seriously—I did not take it into account when I planned for this. And the heat. It's like slogging through a hot spring every time you want to move. I'm sure my hair is just a wonder right now, and the look I get from someone I assume is a judge—with her fancy chef coat and professorial black-rimmed glasses—confirms it. Sweat is glinting off her dark brown skin, shiny and wet under the kitchen lights, so I know she feels it, too. But her hair is not a massive half-purple feat of engineering right now, so point 1 to the disapproving professor judge.

When I finally get in there, Dr. Lavell, inexplicably, is there already, not a hair out of place. Perhaps I judged the bun too quickly. Apart from the sweat that dampens her skin and shirt, too, she looks like she just teleported here.

"For this challenge," Dr. Lavell says, "you will, given the ingredients around you, re-create the food you wrote your entrance essay on. That will be mostly different for each of you, and we have record of what you wrote about, so do not cheat. For those of you who chose foods to write about that take more than thirty minutes to cook, you may draw three dishes randomly from the bowl in front of Dr. Freeman and choose the one with which you are most comfortable."

Several students head to the front, and Dr. Lavell allows them all to choose, with the exception of one blonde girl, to whom she says, "If you cannot re-create a cake into cupcakes in thirty minutes, Ms. Richards, we might have a problem."

The girl blinks at the floor and heads back to her work station with the rest of us.

Thank the lord this is a teaching kitchen, so there are a million different ovens and stovetops for us all.

"Our judges," says Dr. Lavell, "are Doctors Freeman, Pearce, and Kapoor. We will make proper introductions tomorrow. But for now . . ." She pauses and glances up at the clock. "Begin."

Hell yes. Grilled cheese. The problem with having half an hour to make it will be waiting long enough—too early and the cheese will harden. So I take my time. I cross the sudden madhouse of a kitchen amid clangs and crashes so loud it's like a battlefield in here, but I do so lazily. Slow, because there's no reason to rush. I pick a nice, heavy-bottomed skillet and grab a loaf of French bread from the pantry. Cut that too soon and the bread will go crusty. This dish requires me to be sluggish.

As I make my way to the refrigerator, I see Reid, head inside it. He glances at me when he pops back out, eyes shining. "Still moving slow, Purple Haze?"

"The best things in life are not about speed, my friend."

His mouth jerks in an almost-smile, then he says, "Need something?"

"Butter. And provolone."

He tosses me a stick of butter. Twenty minutes sitting close enough to a stove will soften it perfectly.

"Not seeing any provolone here," he says.

"That can't be right." I furrow my brow and push past him into the fridge. He just shrugs and walks off, quickly—whatever he's making is clearly going to take him the whole thirty. The fridge about levels me with a blast of cold air, and the hum buzzes louder and louder in my ears the longer I look. It's stuffed with everything— greens, fruits, herbs, cheeses. I rummage through the stack of cheese about a million times and find nothing. He was right. There's no provolone here. Shit. Shit, oh shit. The whole magic of this is in the cheese!

Suddenly my heart is racing and my palms are sweating—over *cheese*—and how could they not have this? Like what, do they not have *milk* either, in this professional kitchen? *Sorry, we're out of bread here! Nah, we didn't think of stocking salt!*

"Hey, the rest of us need the fridge, too. Time's up." Some jerk guy behind me.

I grit my teeth and yank out some mozzarella and muenster, then rage my way over to my table.

"Twenty minutes!" Lavell calls out.

Have I been moving that slow? Crap. I set my butter pretty close to this impossibly confident-looking girl's hot burner, close enough that I have to really watch it to make sure it doesn't liquefy and run all over the counter. Then I chop at the French bread, but that does nothing but mutilate it, so I force myself to calm the hell down and saw it thinly. If I can't make my dish with provolone, I'm going to get *this* right. The bread comes out perfectly and now the time really is ticking, so I slam my skillet down on the burner, letting it heat, and spread the butter on each piece of bread.

"You okay?" says Reid, and I can do nothing but snarl at him. He laughs and goes back to whatever it is he's making, which I'm sure they had *all* the ingredients for.

I shake my head as I toast the first two sandwiches, stuck together with freaking mozzarella and muenster, and for a second, the smell of butter calms me. This is my happy place. It is. It's fine. I shut my eyes, absorbing a million sweet and savory smells, until one rises above the rest: smoke.

My eyes fly open and I see it's coming from my pan. CURSE BUTTER; CURSE IT TO THE DEPTHS. Half my stuff is burned and eight minutes are left on the clock. So

I rinse out the skillet, hissing as the skin of my arm rubs against it—and it feels like fire. The pretty, absurdly calm and confident girl beside me doesn't look up from her powdered sugar, but says, "You okay?"

I throw out a hurried, "Yeah," almost annoyed that anyone noticed. But not enough that I can do anything but like her automatically.

I turn back to my newly clean skillet, ignoring my arm, and frantically will it to heat again. I crowd the thing, so the edges of each of my tiny grilled cheeses rub up against each other.

This time, I keep my eyes on them; these absolutely cannot burn. I straighten and flip them, heat from the pan scorching into my burn, and swear so loudly that I'm sure everyone in the room hears me.

"Two minutes!" Lavell yells.

If my brain were on broadcast right now, it would have to be shown on HBO. It's nothing but swear words. They need a full minute to finish cooking. Damn, I should have made some candied bacon to overlay it for plating—

"One minute!"

No time. I toss them onto my four plates and my hands are in the air just as she calls time. I note disasters and masterpieces down the row, and mine could not look more boring. I shouldn't have been so slow at the beginning.

My eyes immediately dart to Reid's plate and narrow instantly. "What kind of cheese is that? On that grilled eggplant?"

He just looks at me, then turns back to Lavell.

"You will receive your evaluations and team assignments tomorrow. Leave your plates where they are.

Judging will typically be conducted publicly, but for this number of students, until you are placed in your teams tomorrow, that will be impossible. So head back to the dorms, and I suggest you get some sleep."

I can't stop thinking about that cheese.

When Reid leaves his table, I see it: provolone. *Leftover* provolone. Scads. Of provolone.

"You asshole," I hiss the second we're back outside.

"Hmm?" He arches a brow and keeps walking.

"The provolone. You said—"

"I said it wasn't in the refrigerator. It wasn't."

"It was in your hand!"

"So you understand."

I can feel the rage bubbling up from my toes to my throat. My head is going to explode.

"Why?" is all I can manage.

"Come on," he says, and the phrase *I'm not here to make friends* flashes through my brain. That's what this is. A competition. And I can play dirty, too.

We are nearing the dorms now. He and I will go our separate ways, thank the lord. And just as he pulls ahead of me, I say a bit too loudly, "Wait until tomorrow, you cocky ass. You won't know what hit you."

He stops straight, then, and waits for me to catch up. "Pumpkin," he says, and I bristle. He leans down and says into my ear, "I will *destroy* you."

# CHAPTER THREE

I am still on fire when I finally crest the stairs and get my room assignment from the woman I assaulted with my BB-8 suitcase earlier. She looks a little pinched when she hands it to me, but not flat-out resentful, which is probably the best I can ask for, foot injuries considered.

I fold the sheet of paper, neat and symmetrically creased, and slide it into my back pocket, then wrestle my bag over the soft carpet down the hall. Room 209. I knock softly just in case, then push the door open. There's someone in there already, back turned to me, and she has claimed the bed by the window. Fine by me; no sun streaming into my face in the morning.

"Hi," I say, and she turns around, mouth ticking up into a smile. Her hair falls in black waves all the way to her waist and she's wearing yoga pants and a magenta ribbed tank that's bright against her brown skin. The confident girl from the kitchen. The one who checked on my burn. She nods at me.

"Hey. How's that arm?"

I laugh, half-embarrassed. "I'll survive. I'm Carter. Looks like we're rooming together?"

"Riya," she says. "What's your specialty, Carter?"

"I'm a skillet kind of girl. Despite what my injury might tell you."

"Oh good," she says. "Should be a while before we have to be at each other's throats then. I am sugar and spice and everything . . . baking. I bake, mostly. And am clearly a poet."

"Clearly."

She laughs and goes back to trying to fluff the pillows on her little bed, which seems like a pretty fruitless endeavor to me. These pillows are pancakes and nothing can be done to force them to rise.

I try to get a hand through my hair and it snags four hundred times. "Humidity," I mumble, and Riya snorts.

"Yeah, it's hell on hair. I assume you hail from the desert? Or the . . . non-swamp?"

"Montana," I say.

"Wow. Mountain woman."

I grin. "Not exactly."

"West Virginia," she says. "Not western Virginia, if you're wondering. West Virginia. It's a state."

I laugh. "I believe you."

She cocks her head, eyeing my unruly hair. "Just embrace it. A little mousse and going out there like you planned it. Best policy for most things, I've found."

I purse my lips when my fingers snag yet again and nod. "I'll give it my best effort."

Then I turn to my side and start the slow, painful process of unpacking as the sun sets. It's vibrant down here, bright pink and blue. It makes the Spanish moss outside look like something out of a fairytale.

I sigh. And hang everything up one by one. The sooner this is done, the sooner I can sleep. Riya is friendly but not a chatterer, which means that in an hour, I can crawl into bed and embrace the quiet and try to get rid of the headache that has been building behind my eyes since I was brutally betrayed by an arrogant boy and a package of provolone.

Morning comes early. It comes particularly early because Riya wakes up practically at sunrise, and she does it to the Avengers theme song, which is both unexpected and very, very loud. I go with her suggestion—embracing the mop of insanity on my head—because it allows me to lie around a little longer. Just a little mousse and brush my teeth, then throw a T-shirt on over my sleep shorts, and I'm padding down the stairs in my socks.

Breakfast starts in five minutes and hell if I was going to take the extra time away from sleep to dress like a human. I follow a group of four girls in front of me who seem to have bonded really quickly, and Riya and I just walk quietly together. These girls look like they know where they're going, and I am certain that I do not. We pass the common room, which is filled with old books and framed by the ancient, dual curved staircases that lead to the dorms, and through a little hallway with bathrooms and mystery rooms on either side. Then the hallway opens up into a tiny cafeteria. Everything in here is tiny. Old. Intimate. I think I like it, until I spot Reid across the way sitting at a filled four-person round table. A sour taste fills my mouth when I realize I just thought the words *Reid* and *intimate* in the same minute, and the scowl on my face is vicious enough to make Riya say, "Wow, you haven't even tried the food yet. It's probably decent; this *is* a cooking school."

"Not the food," I say, and I can't tear my eyes off him. He's just sitting there in these loose plaid pajama pants and an old T-shirt stretched tight over his chest, mouth tilted in this way that has everyone at his table scrambling for his attention. He's amused, but not *really* invested, and it's killing all of them. I hate him and his stupid undercut bedhead and his stupid provolone.

"Oh, I see," she says, and I blink over at her.

"Oh. No. No it's not . . ."

"Okay," says Riya, eyes twinkling.

"Sorry, I don't look at guys like I want to rip their throats out if I'm interested."

"Suit yourself," says Riya. "You and I must be laying eyes on *very different boys* because hello."

I roll my eyes and step into the food line, glancing over my shoulder at him one more time, and this time, he's looking back.

I feel a jolt all the way down to my toes, because that cocky little smirk that seems like a fixture on his face is gone. And the three people at his table are all clearly trying to get his attention, but the asshole is looking at me. After half a second, he blinks away and I focus on loading up my plate with French toast and powdered sugar and some of the ripest-looking fruit I've ever seen.

I follow Riya to a little table in the corner and slam my plate down with more force than is strictly necessary. She kind of jumps and just looks at me with her wide brown eyes. "What's your deal?"

"Reid Yamada. He's just an asshole."

Riya raises an eyebrow and takes a long drink of her orange juice. "Okayyyy."

"He took my freaking provolone yesterday on purpose. In the first challenge. It's just . . . I mean that's really shitty, and who cares. But it's shitty and I'm still mad about it."

Riya says, "Be mad. Channel it. *Use your hate.*" Then an Indian boy I don't recognize but she obviously does sits beside her.

I open my mouth to say something terrible about Reid and Riya says, "Eat your toast. Plot the downfall of the Iron Throne later."

That startles a laugh from me and I focus on my food. It's still cafeteria food, but it's *good* cafeteria food, so I'm happy.

"This is Will, by the way," she says, nodding at the boy next to her, who I've just now noticed is extremely attractive. He's got glasses and a smile that makes my knees go a little weak. Thank the lord I'm sitting. "Also from West Virginia."

"You guys know each other?"

"Yeah," says Will.

I say, "Are you, like, together?"

Riya starts laughing immediately, face going red, and Will lets out a little cough. "No," he says. "We met at this thing our parents were going to at the India Center, and then just started hanging out. We started cooking together when we realized we were both into it. That's it, though."

"I'm Carter," I say.

"What's up."

"What did you make yesterday?" I ask them both.

Will says, "I happened to kill it on something I grew up with. Chicken biryani."

Riya mouths it as the same time he says it and he wrinkles his nose, then flicks hers.

"Ouch!"

"Well," he says.

"You're obsessed with that dish."

He raises an eyebrow. "And you've been paying very close attention to my food habits. Are you obsessed with *me*?"

She goes bright red again and rolls her eyes, shoving him. I suppress a grin.

"I made beignets." She sighs and raises her hand to her forehead in a mock swoon.

"How could one lose on beignets?"

"Right?" She spares one last scowl for Will, then looks back at me. "You?"

"Grilled cheese," I say.

She laughs then. "Without cheese? That *is* unfortunate."

"Well. I substituted. But yeah. A problem." I laugh, then, because Riya is laughing and the absurdity of it isn't lost on me. Riya's laugh is kind of infectious.

"Well, just make sure today in the kitchen—" Riya pauses and stares at me meaningfully, and I look back.

"What?"

"Uh."

"Let me take your plate." Reid's voice startles me badly enough that I jump, and apple juice sloshes over the side of my cup.

I narrow my eyes. "What?"

"Your fruit plate. It's empty."

I snort. "Why? Planning on poisoning it when I'm not looking?"

"Well it's empty so that wouldn't be very effective."

My eyes narrow further. They are slits and I am *pissed.*

"Did you seriously walk all the way over here just to take my fruit plate?"

Reid's lips thin into a line and he runs a hand through the wild tuft of hair on top of his head, thumb brushing the shaved sides. "Yeah. That and . . ." He glances over at Riya, who is doing a terrible job of pretending not to eavesdrop, and Will, who is not pretending not to at all. Reid looks back at me and his fingers drop to brush my elbow. "Can I talk to you?" He inclines his head toward the hall.

Riya takes a bite of her cinnamon roll, and it is clear that chewing is an effort. She's not even faking disinterest anymore.

I blow out a breath through my nose and bite into my French toast with butter pecan syrup. I do not hurry. Let the jerk wait.

He does.

"Lord," I breathe, then I stand in a huff. "Fine."

"What the hell?" Will breathes just before I'm out of earshot.

And I follow Reid out into the empty, close hallway.

I force myself not to look straight at him, because he may be Satan's cheese-loving stepchild, but the darkness of his eyes is frustratingly distracting. So I take in the old burgundy carpet on the floor, the flowered wallpaper on the walls wherever there isn't wood. Anything but him.

"I wanted to say I was . . ."

I glance up at his face. "Yeah?" I do my best to make my voice sound flat. Disinterested. Removed completely, which is not my way. But it is today.

Reid swallows and glances up at the ceiling then back down at my face. "I was an asshole yesterday."

"Yes."

"Like, a giant asshole. I shouldn't have taken your stuff. Just heat in the kitchen or whatever. Competition. You get it, right?"

"I don't need this," I say. "You don't owe me anything. Not like we're friends."

"I know."

"You know?"

He raises an eyebrow. "Yes, I know we're not friends. Yes, I know I don't owe you. But yes, I also know it was shitty. Okay?"

My instinct is to say, "Fine! All is forgiven!" But I think so much of that comes from my difficult-to-control desire to run my hands through his unruly hair—on a purely physical level—that I don't trust it. My own body has betrayed me. I school my features into boredom and cross my arms. "Why'd you do it?" I say.

And now he is flustered. Reid Yamada is full of surprises. In the last eighteen hours, I had deemed him unflusterable.

"I don't know," he says. "I just . . ." Then he kind of furrows his brow and straightens, and his voice changes into something matter-of-fact, resolute. "I want to win this. I saw an opportunity. I took it. I shouldn't have. It was a mistake."

"A mistake."

"Yes."

"And you're what?"

Now it's Reid's turn to narrow his eyes. He stands taller—lord, he looks tall in this hallway—and when he moves, I can smell the scent of syrup and waffles coming off him. "Come on," he says.

"You. Are. What?"

Reid says nothing, he just hardens his jaw. So I turn and grab the door handle. He reaches out, hand gentle but very present on my elbow. I turn.

"I'm sorry," he says. He grits it out like a foreign language, like something he has never had the occasion to say before. And the syllables sound wrong in his mouth.

I purse my lips and look down at the ground. He's sorry. Maybe being this pissed over provolone is unreasonable. Maybe I'm being ridiculous. So I say, "Okay."

"Are we good?" he says.

I scrape my teeth over my bottom lip. "I don't get why it matters. But yeah. Yeah, we're fine." It tastes like a lie the moment it lands on my tongue, but it's said. It's done. We're good.

I push back into the little dining hall and, for whatever reason, I almost feel more angry than I did this morning. But then Reid waits at his table until I'm done eating and sweeps my plate and fruit bowl away to get them washed, and comes back with a fresh cup of juice, so it's unreasonable. He's being nice. He looks like he would rather be doing anything else, but he's clearly feeling guilty because resting bitch face or not, he's being *so nice*.

Will has already left the table when I get back. But Riya stands with me after we finish breakfast and we head in the direction of our room to get dressed before the first challenge. When we see the team lists have been posted, we stop briefly to examine them.

Twelve on one, twelve on the other. Will is on the other team. Riya is on my team, and Reid isn't. Who gives a shit? I forgave him. We're cool. We're fine. It's fine.

But the cool rage is still flickering in my chest even when I shut the door to my room and don't have to think about him at all.

# CHAPTER FOUR

This kitchen feels hotter today, which probably has something to do with all the nervous energy crackling through everyone. We're all in aprons, buzzing with anticipation. Sweating—partially because it's Savannah, and partially because there are literally too many cooks in this kitchen and there's just a lot of pressure and body heat. I'm suddenly worried I didn't put on enough deodorant. Which is concerning. But there's no subtle way to check, and either way I should be pretty easily disguised by the ten other people in this room who clearly didn't.

Dr. Kapoor stands and says, "Chefs, you will be judged individually, based on your dishes from last night, on your performance we observe in this kitchen, and as a group. For this challenge, you will be working in your assigned teams."

Everyone glances around at their team members, like we haven't been doing that since the lists were posted. But I'm looking at the competition. Because Reid is staring at me, dark eyebrows raised. There's an almost-smile on his lips and suddenly I'm on fire. Because here we are in this kitchen where he intentionally screwed me over less than twenty-four hours ago, and he may be sorry, but I can't stand the injustice of it.

I'll have to, though. This is not about him; it's about me, and that scholarship, and our team. I narrow my eyes at him and look back at Dr. Kapoor.

"You will present your dishes when the time runs down, after which we will discuss. Three of you will be returning home tomorrow."

A ripple of nerves runs down my spine, because what if. What if, what if.

What if I get sent home tomorrow and it's like this whole thing was a fluke? Then I'll know I should never have been here, never belonged here, it had been a total waste to apply, which was what my brain was screaming at me through every sentence I typed in the essay.

*This is not for you. When have things like this ever been for you?*

And I'll have to go back there and face everyone who's too nice to say, *Dream smaller, kiddo.*

What if.

Nervous energy rumbles through the group as fast as it runs through me. Come on, deodorant, do what you were made to do.

"You will have forty minutes," Dr. Kapoor says. "Forty minutes to prepare an appetizer, a main course, and a dessert."

"Forty minutes?" Riya squeaks beside me.

"We'll have to split up," I mumble to her, and a boy with dirty blond surfer hair and shockingly pale skin leans in to listen. "Four on desserts, four on apps, four on main."

"You will be given three ingredients. One per course. You may choose which course you would like to use each in, but they *must* be divided so that one mystery ingredient appears in each. Is that understood?"

A murmured chorus of *yeses* and *yes, sirs* goes up from us all.

"Open your boxes. The three ingredients for this round are: black garlic."

"What the hell is that?" I say under my breath, and Surfer Dude tosses his hair out of his eyes and smirks. He knows exactly what it is.

"Bok choy."

Okay. Okay, bok choy I think I can take.

"And jackfruit."

I raise an eyebrow at Riya, who says, "I know jack shit about jackfruit."

I laugh.

Dr. Kapoor looks down at the timer in his hand.

"Time begins . . . now."

And the kitchen devolves into chaos.

Everyone is shouting over each other on the red team, clawing for control, and on blue, it's totally quiet. We're frozen.

I glance back over my shoulder, eyes landing on Reid. Some tiny girl on his team says, "So, bok choy. Stir fry maybe?"

She looks straight at him and Reid hisses, "I don't know how the hell to cook bok choy."

The girl goes bright red and I raise my eyebrows, and Reid's gaze lands on mine. It's burning up.

31

"I think—" I start, but then Bowl Cut Surfer steps smoothly in.

"We'll divide into three groups of four. You, you, you, and you." He sections off one group, then another, then steps in with mine. I am instantly frustrated, but his voice is so smooth and commanding that everyone is listening, and he took my idea. I'm sure it's an idea half of us had, and I'm sure it's what Team Red will do, but still. "You guys, take apps and the bok choy. Dessert, take the jackfruit. We'll take the main course and black garlic."

No one protests, but I say, voice way too quiet in a kitchen that, on Team B's half, is ridiculously loud, "Jackfruit in the dessert is kind of non-risky, though, right? Like creatively, maybe we should—"

"Get going, guys," he says, and I clench my teeth, fist curling at my side.

"We need to at least discuss the freaking dishes so we know they complement each other."

"Fine," he says, spinning and looking down his nose at me. "You go poll everyone, the three of us will start actually *cooking*. We're low on time."

I'm actually vibrating with rage when the group splits and he heads for the food. I don't even know what we're making. "Listen!" I say.

"What?"

It doesn't matter; the whole group is just doing whatever they want to do at this point, but it's so frustrating. "What's your name?"

"Andrew."

"Well. Andrew. What are we even going to ma—"

"Go get the balsamic vinegar and parsley. And you"—he nods at Riya—"get me some scallops. I'll heat the pan." The other girl with us heads straight for the refrigerator so this is clearly a recipe she's familiar with. And I want to argue, but there's no time. Dammit. *Dammit.* I blow out a breath and just follow his instructions. Even if maybe he's wrong.

He shouldn't even be cooking the scallops yet; it's too early. They'll go rubbery. But I can bring that up later. Right now, I'm an errand girl. I need balsamic and parsley. I shove my way across the kitchen as smells start wafting around and get the parsley without a problem. I shoulder-bump Reid when I reach for the balsamic vinegar and he says, "Find what you need?"

"You think I'm telling you what I need?"

He lets out this little laugh and says, "Fair."

And I snatch the vinegar, then head back to the stove. There's already butter sizzling in the pan.

"Don't start these yet," I say. "You'll—"

"I know how to cook scallops, good lord."

Riya puts a hand on my elbow then shoots a glare at the guy. "Show a little respect, Boy Band."

Andrew cocks his head, jaw clenched. Then he just rolls his eyes and goes back to the sauté pan. I get to chopping garlic hard enough that I am briefly concerned I might slip and whack off a finger. But I control it. Focus.

I am chopping black garlic.

This is important.

I am here doing something that matters, and who cares if some guy is being the worst? Riya gets to coating the scallops in whatever spices and the other girl in our group is just standing there, worshiping Tall, Blond, and Arrogant.

The timer starts to really run down, and the smells in the kitchen are all running together. Everyone is moving so quickly, and I feel like I'm doing *nothing*, and in this instant, I am pure fury. Because Andrew is doing everything, and there's no time to coordinate our dishes so everything is random, and no one will listen to me so I'm sure I am more than underwhelming the judging panel. And on top of everything, my stupid grilled cheese from last night was probably not a perfect ten. I could be going home. Everything is out of my control and I could be going home.

Andrew starts cooking the scallops.

I have literally nothing to do. So I get out the plates.

I glance over at Team Red, who is working so smoothly; they're like greased cogs, a big, efficient machine. And Reid is bending over his counter, making these chocolate cages that are so perfect I want to cry. He has this furrow between his eyebrows, jaw clamped shut. So focused I bet I could stare at him like this for minutes on end and he wouldn't even notice.

His fingers are moving with absolute precision over the chocolate, and yeah . . . it's flawless.

Meanwhile, someone over here seems to have gotten the bright idea to make jackfruit ice cream and gotten it out too late so it's jackfruit butter, basically, and Andrew is doing what does seem like a beautiful job on those scallops. I have no idea what our appetizer even is.

"Two minutes! Start looking at plates, people!"

That, I've gotten down. I am the master of the plates.

Everyone starts plating. And once again, I am left to do nothing with my hands. I mentally kick myself for not being louder, not being authoritative. I wish I stood out as much as the purple in my hair.

I hate feeling powerless.

Less than.

And here we are.

I catch a glimpse of Reid, finishing those last cages. He sets them gently over these little cakes someone brought him, on a single plate to carry them to the presentation area, and yesterday's Reid flashes in a wicked photograph behind my eyes.

*Pumpkin, I will destroy you.*

My lips curls with my hands.

I am not powerless.

Reid brushes right past me, and I don't think about it. I just move. Make like I'm reaching for another utensil in front of me, but slide my foot just in front of his.

He stumbles. And for one split-second, I think he's going to recover.

He doesn't.

Reid's eyes widen and his mouth makes a little *O*, just before he, and every one of those cakes and cages, crashes to the ground.

I lean back.

The kitchen goes briefly silent.

Then there is an absolute flurry of activity. Our food is going on plates, Team B is *frantic*. And I cannot decide between feeling elated and guilty.

Dr. Kapoor calls time.

We stand in a group by our dishes.

Andrew, of course, takes charge of ours, introducing the most disjointed meal of all time. A thick Thai bok choy soup, black garlic scallops, jackfruit ice cream. A curl of shame rises in my stomach. The food looks good on its own, at least.

The judges take bites of each. "Altogether this meal is not cohesive. Nothing . . . nothing fits. But individually, this soup is delicious, truly. The scallops are overdone—"

"Mine were slightly undercooked."

Dr. Freeman says, "My scallops were done to perfection. But can we talk about the ice cream?"

And it is at that point that their voices start to fade. Because I can feel it. I can feel Reid's eyes boring holes in the side of my head. I grit my teeth and curl my fingers, then uncurl them. Do not look. I cannot look over at him. I cannot let him have this.

But it almost hurts not to.

I break my rule. I look.

Reid is practically smoking out his ears. He's got chocolate and crumbs all over his apron, and I can see him working hard trying to control his breathing. His jaw is hard, nostrils flared. His gaze is hot and wicked, and I swear he wants to walk right over to our side of the kitchen and put his hands around my throat.

I stare back at him. Don't let him see your guilt. Don't let him stare you down. My face wears a mask of boredom and I turn back to the judges. They are what matters.

Our reception is mixed. Because Andrew is good at commanding control of a room and terrible at knowing what exactly to do once he gets it.

The red team presents their dishes—Will takes the bok choy stir fry over crostinis, and this tiny pale boy with Harry Potter glasses takes the black garlic tofu, both of which fit perfectly with one another. And they look incredible. They smell so good, I want to snatch a plate from the judges and devour it all.

Then Reid steps forward. He's sweating. "Your . . . your dessert is a jackfruit reduction. It was originally going to be Chinese egg cakes and chocolate cages with a jackfruit reduction drizzle." He swallows hard, stands straighter. I can see his fingers tapping at his sides.

I do not feel guilty. I refuse to feel guilty. He started this.

"Unfortunately," he says, "as I was moving to plate the dessert, I tripped. So what you have is the . . . the jackfruit. Reduction."

Cocky, self-assured Reid. Reduced to pure nerves.

My chest squeezes and I blink past it.

The judges eat. They love the first two dishes, but the lack of dessert is going to screw them. Every one of us in this room knows it. And every one of us knows they would have won this round without it.

We are all dismissed for the evening.

I walk as quickly as possible out of the kitchen after I strip out of my apron, hoping to outpace Reid. Maybe he won't confront me at all. Maybe he thinks this was his screw-up.

I cross the grass in record time and breathe a sigh of relief as I hit the doors.

But Reid's hand is at my arm, and I spin around, back to the brick wall of the old dorm.

"Are you serious?" Reid says. There is still sweat beaded up around his forehead. His hair is sticky and damp, falling over his eyes.

He is standing so close, eyes pure anger. Anger and . . . embarrassment.

I fold my arms over my chest. "About what?" I flick my eyes to the ground and I know I look guilty as hell.

Reid just blinks down at me, and I can feel the fury radiating off his chest, flames on the side of his face.

Then he makes this scoffing noise that gets me feeling frustratingly guilty, shakes his head, and walks away.

# CHAPTER FIVE

I have elected to eat in my room, because it's pizza, and that's a total eat-it-in-your-dorm kind of thing.

We both change into pajamas, and Riya says, "Cool if a couple girls come over? Not to like stay up and throw a rager or whatever, just yeah. Hanging out."

My eyebrows shoot up. "Is *everyone* here from West Virginia?"

She laughs. "No. Only one I know from before is Will."

"So you've made friends here *already*? Good lord, what is your life?"

She laughs again and shrugs, this dainty little maneuver on her somehow, and I settle onto my bed, because people can be here, but I am free of my bra already and no one is getting me to put it back on.

I will remain in my natural habitat: this bed surrounded by shitty dorm room pillows, as the lord intended.

"What do you want to do?" asks Riya, and I furrow my brow, then glance over at her.

"What do you mean?"

"Like with food. You graduate, what do you do?"

I sigh, and it comes out embarrassingly dreamy. "It's not realistic," I say. Like I need the qualifier. But it's . . . I mean, it's not. You have to be Someone Big to do what I want to do and I am Someone Perfectly Medium. "I want to go somewhere really cool. Paris or Rome or Tokyo, somewhere with amazing food. Learn a few things, a couple specialty courses? Then come back to the US, a newly minted Julia Child, and own my own restaurant. In New York. L.A. Denver. Somewhere kickass."

Riya whistles. "See the world and own your own place. You are in for some sleepless nights, my friend."

I shrug. I don't tell her that the last vacation I was on was to a lake forty minutes away and we slept in a little tent, and that apart from this one time I visited my grandparents in Nebraska, I don't remember ever leaving Montana. Because my childhood was good—it's been good and it still is—but we barely have money for rent, and sometimes we don't even have that. I can never remember having money for an actual vacation. I don't say I want to see the world because I haven't even seen my own country and, by now, my own country has kind of lost its mystique. I don't say that I know that's out of the realm of reasonable. I just smile and say, "I don't mind giving up sleep. What about you?"

"I want to work at a top bakery. Maybe go see the world, maybe stay, I don't know. Probably not in West Virginia. But I'm a science kind of girl; I love the precision of baking. This much flour and this much baking soda creates this reaction and at this altitude the air reacts with the dough just this way."

"Sounds like you want to be a chemist."

She says, "Same thing."

I smile. I love cooking because of the messiness. Grease is going to pop and burn you and sometimes stuff will turn out and sometimes it won't. And you just throw it all in the skillet and kind of see what comes together. I love the uncertainty of it all. You have to *master* it for food to turn out for you.

"My grandpa cooked," I say. "Both of my parents are kind of terrible at it, and when Grandpa died, Mom had a really hard time with it. So I kind of just slid into that opportunity to start making dinner for everyone because I'd done it with Grandpa since I was super little. And seriously, to call what either of my parents ever made from scratch 'edible' would be, like, high praise." She giggles. "So I'd been in love with the whole experience since I was five and got my first wrist burn from a sizzling pan, and when I had the excuse to take care of everyone, this is what I picked. It's like . . . part of me, or something? Which sounds so cheesy. I just heard it."

"Not cheesy. Baking is kind of an anti-anxiety thing for me, I think. Always calmed me down when I was freaking out over a test or one of my friends being a bitch. Betty Crocker would never let me down. Not if I combined the ingredients *just so*. It's been me and my Easy-Bake Oven since I could walk."

"Easy-Bake Oven, oh man," I say.

"The most mythical lightbulb ever created to cook food."

I'm grinning just thinking about it. I swear, sometimes my thoughts surrounding food and the utensils with which one makes it are more romantic than anything else.

And here it's like, so are everyone else's. They all love this so much, want it bad enough to give up a whole summer here. And I guarantee, *no one* here views it as giving anything up. I bet they all write sonnets to butter and caramelized onions in their sleep. They all get heart eyes for macarons and flutters in their stomachs for a perfectly braised lamb shank. These are my people.

My people, who I will have to try to brutally destroy in every round of competition from here on out.

Someone knocks on our door and Riya says, "Come in!" And I shit you not, three different girls walk in and Riya hugs *all* of them like she knows them. Three girls. In like twenty-four hours. How is that even possible?

There's this tall black girl name Tess with square glasses and an amazing afro; a short, round girl with a southern accent named Addie; and a particularly pale girl named Patricia who has light blue braces and freckles on her nose. They say hi to me, but I refuse to move from my blanket cocoon, so pretty quickly, all three of them head over to Riya's bed.

Addie snuck in a little alcohol somehow, and normally I would be interested but tonight I'm exhausted. Partially because it's just been . . . a lot. And thinking about Grandpa's cooking, and then Mom and Dad back in Montana, well. It has me suddenly missing everyone, bad enough it almost hurts. Like I'm some little kid who can't handle a sleepover.

I shoot both my parents a quick, nonchalant, *Miss you love you* text, and Mom hits me back with three lines of emojis, which both eases the kiddish pang in my chest and sharpens it.

The other complication, the other thing making me want to shut out all these nice girls invading my room, is that even though I shouldn't, I feel bad about Reid. And I can't stop thinking about the look on his face when he just sighed and walked past me in the quad.

So they laugh and drink and whatever, and it's fine. But I pass out to a lovely chorus of guilt in my head. Reid scowls me into sleep.

# CHAPTER SIX

"The winning team this week should come as no surprise," says Dr. Pearce, and it is only now that I realize he has a British accent, which I can only assume is because I've never actually heard the man speak. He's gained minimum fifteen hotness points just from the way he forms his vowels. I blink down at the ground to get that out of my head (until he speaks again) and look up.

We're all gathered outside in this little amphitheater for judging; we are gonna be spending so much time in the kitchen that they kind of look for reasons to gather us together outside it, so here we are, sitting on stone, breathing in actual water from the sky.

"The blue team presented us some rather flavorful and creative dishes, albeit with some inconsistencies in the main course, though their meal was not entirely cohesive. But, while their overall meal had several small issues which the judges discussed both with you all and in private deliberation, the red team ultimately only presented us with two courses. Red team, while your jackfruit reduction had a lovely texture and flavor, a drizzle of a sauce is, unfortunately, not enough to qualify as a dessert."

A grumble rises up from half the students, though Riya and two of the girls from last night are basically vibrating with happiness in their seats around me. I feel another twist of guilt wrench my stomach. I wasn't just sabotaging Reid; it was his whole *team*. They'll eat him alive for this. If he makes it past this week.

"Three students will be going home this evening. Before we commence, I want to say that it is an honor having you all here, and it is with my deepest regret that we must, alas, send several of you back to pack. Blue team, in tonight's judging, you are all safe."

A lone whoop slices through the night, and I don't have to look to know it's Andrew. I can't even think his name without rolling my eyes.

"Abigil Petrovi, Ingrid Evers, Will Malik,"—Riya sits up straight—"Peter Williams, Reid Yamada, and Timothy Parker. If all of you would please step forward."

There's a shuffling, and a ton of clearly angry grumbles over on the red side. We naturally separated ourselves. In the dorms, we can be unified. But out here, it's a battlefield.

"When it came to the individual challenge, one of you here before us had far and away the best dish of the night. You are safe. It was flavorful, perfectly done, one of the most expertly crafted meals I've had the pleasure of tasting, particularly on the first night, since I began judging four years ago." Riya is mouthing the words *chicken biryani* right along with Dr. Pearce as he names the dish and says, "Will Malik, congratulations. You will be staying with us another week. Well done."

Will's shoulders drop in relief and he scans the crowd, smile wide and bright, for Riya, who gives him a thumbs-up when his gaze catches hers. Then he goes back to sit, practically falling back into his seat.

"Ingrid," he says, "while your teamwork in the kitchen on the group dish was admirable, I'm afraid your individual dish was well conceived, but rather dry, and we all wanted to see more flavor from you in the buttercream on top of the cupcake. We appreciate having gotten the chance to work with you, but you will need to head home this evening."

Ingrid glances at the floor but clenches her jaw and handles it.

It goes like that until Peter has been sent home, too, and the last people standing are Timothy and Reid.

"Reid," says Dr. Pearce, and I hold my breath. I didn't actually want to get him sent *home*; I wanted vengeance. It really was supremely shitty, what he did to me, and I don't think I'm totally off-base wanting a little vindication. But guilt is dissolving me from the inside. They all took a major hit. Because of me.

And now maybe Reid is going home.

And *going home* doesn't just mean leaving. It means going to the airport, hanging out by the gate on standby at who knows what ungodly hour, for a flight you pray you will not get kicked off of. The school has a deal with the little airport that gets us flights for cheap, at the cost of certainty in one's flight and convenience in the time it takes off. It's like an extra degree of humiliation.

I'm tapping my fingers so fast on the stone seat in the amphitheater that Riya looks at me and raises an eyebrow, but I can't hear what she whispers because I am completely focused on Dr. Pearce. And on Reid's back. He's standing so straight, fists clenched at his sides, as Dr. Pearce goes over each of their individual dishes, saying how Reid's was utterly masterful and Timothy's borscht was oddly textured and low on flavor, but it was such an ambitious choice that they were considering giving him a pass. The thing is, everyone knows Reid made some of the most beautiful chocolate cages of all time, and everyone knows he was the one who dropped them. So what it comes down to is, does it send him home?

I'm grinding my teeth—I can feel them squeaking against each other. But I can't quit.

"Ultimately, we have decided that one of you should get another chance," says Dr. Pearce, and I want to shake him. Because *who*? Who? My body was not built to withstand such guilt; it is built to last under heavy intake of butter and cheese and ballroom dance via YouTube tutorial, when I'm not feeling too dorky to admit I'm into that. But guilt—guilt is its weakness.

"Mr. Yamada," he says, and my whole body tenses. All my bones are going to snap right here, right now, and I will be the first student in history to explode into a pile of bloody goo during judging. "We have determined that clumsiness, while something we do not plan to be overly tolerant of in the future, is not a determining factor in regard to one's culinary skills, and it would be a waste of your potential to send you home for faulty footwork. Do not let it happen again."

"Yes, sir," says Reid, and I can hear the shaky relief in his voice.

I practically liquefy down into the stone. I am the Wicked Witch of the Midwest—I'm melting.

Riya gives me a bizarre look for the second time tonight and I don't even summon the will to pay attention.

There are a few sniffles from the eliminated contestants and I grit my teeth to ward off the guilt, but dammit, if they're going home already, they would have gone home eventually.

I repeat that to myself silently as I stew here in this semi-secret shame. And have to force myself not to look at Reid, then stand up and confess it all right here, right now.

Dr. Freeman stands and says, "Go enjoy the rest of your night, competitors. We'll see you in the kitchens tomorrow at ten a.m."

We disperse. Except Reid, who is sitting there, face on his knees, hands clasped behind his neck. No one sat with him during judging, I realize, which is a far cry from where he was at breakfast yesterday morning—surrounded by people just begging for his attention. I stand and am about walk off with Riya and her friends, a group which now includes Will, because we currently exist in that lull between judging and a new challenge, which means we can invoke a temporary peace treaty.

But dammit again. Curse my brain. I cannot stop looking at Reid. He looks like someone literally poked a hole in him and deflated him. And the guilt is spidering everywhere in me now; I can't contain it. I definitely cannot physically ignore it.

I brush my hand over Riya's shoulder and say, "I'll catch up with you guys later, okay?"

She frowns but says, "Yeah. See you later," and then they disappear and it is just Reid and me in the huge, quiet amphitheater. Nothing but Georgia insects, which I assume are all twice the size of Montana insects, whirring and buzzing and quietly cricketing in the trees that wind their way through campus.

It's getting dark now, so everything feels dramatic. Like we're on *Survivor*, or contestants in the Hunger Games, not a cooking show.

Every time you shift on these stone benches, it practically echoes.

So when I stand, I'm sure he hears it. And when I start toward him, I'm sure he hears that, too. He doesn't look up, though, even when I'm right beside him. Just sits there like a dead balloon, long fingers digging into the nape of his neck.

"Reid."

"What. The hell," he says into his own knees, "do you want?"

"Dude, come on—"

He barks out a laugh, then actually looks at me, and it's so sharp it physically hurts. "Come *on*? Come on? Really? Do you get what you did, Carter?"

I take a step backward, arms folded across my chest, and he stands.

"I know I might have overreacted a little—"

"A little? Carter, you got three of my team members sent home and you *know* we would have won if you hadn't pulled such a dirty—"

"Whoa," I say. "You started this. You were the one who screwed me over when I hadn't done anything to you."

"Yeah, barely. You had to substitute some cheese; big whoop. I didn't physically hurt you—"

"Yeah, we should get you to the ER for tripping, Reid—"

"—and I didn't humiliate you in front of everyone. Do you get that my whole damn team hates me right now? Do you get that no one will speak to me? I'm a leper; there's like a ten-foot radius around Reid Yamada, beyond which no red team member will venture."

"I'm sure they'll get past it."

He narrows his eyes and his nostrils flare lightly. "So not even an apology? This is all I get?" He takes a step closer to me, hands at his hip bones, and it's just like it was in the hall. We are outside, in this empty cavern of space, but suddenly it's hot and everything feels extremely close and extremely . . . like I'm caught in his orbit somehow and we're the only two in a tiny room.

I see his jaw tighten when he swallows, the slightest flex in his bicep when he shifts his arm and digs his fingers into his bones, the stretch of the worn fabric of his *Avatar: The Last Airbender* T-shirt.

I open my mouth to apologize, to say I did more damage than I planned to, that I really am sorry, and can we call a truce? But he's just so smug and cocky and pissed that suddenly I don't want to. He's looking down at me because he has to, because he's at least half a foot taller than me, but the stone in his eyes makes me feel like even if I had five inches on him, he would still find a way to look down his nose at me.

I feel bad. But he started this, I didn't. He feels like shit for letting his team down? He should. He made his bed. I lock my jaw and lift my chin.

"You asked for this," I say.

"I said I was sorry."

"That didn't change what you did."

"You want me to get a damn time machine? I am not the Doctor; I don't have one at my disposal."

My heart flutters traitorously at the sudden and unexpected casual geekdom, but I force it to return to its cold, dark state and say, "Then no. I'm not sorry."

Reid puffs out a laugh and looks up at the dark, sparkling sky. He's quiet for long enough that I think maybe he won't tell me what he's thinking at all. Then he finally says, "Fine." His mouth curls up. "That how you want to play with me, sweetheart?"

He looks right back at me and I feel the weight of his stare like a physical, tangible thing.

"You were the one who started the game, Reid."

Reid's eyes narrow.

He gives me this wicked smile and stretches his hand out to me. I shake it.

He says, "Then let's play."

# CHAPTER SEVEN

"You will have ninety minutes to complete this challenge," Dr. Kapoor's clear voice rings out, and my immediate reaction is relief—because no weird baskets of ingredients, twice the time we had last challenge. The next response is crippling fear.

Twice the time and no bizarre basket means something impossible is coming.

I clench my hands at my sides and stare straight ahead. I plan to ignore Reid completely, though that's barely possible. I can feel him over there, smirking at the judges, like he's won already.

He doesn't even know what we're making.

Part of me is hoping that his little declaration of war yesterday won't stand, and that we can just move on with our lives and actually compete. In the school-sanctioned kind of way. But the other part of me can feel it, even from here. That confidence radiating off him isn't because he's just so cocky that he can't imagine failing, even without any information at all. He's cocky because he's planning to get revenge on me.

I curl my fists tighter, short nails digging into my palms. Whatever. I'll just have to pay very careful attention. I'm sure as hell not going to go after him again, not after I about drowned in the guilt last night. I'm playing to actually *win* today, thank you very much.

"Dr. Freeman," says Dr. Kapoor, "if you would be so kind."

Dr. Freeman steps out from behind the judging table, producing a giant bowl from under it. Her heels click on the floor when she holds it out to Dr. Kapoor.

"You will be making desserts today, chefs," he says, and Riya's face beside me breaks out into a wide smile. That's her sweet spot.

Pun not intended.

Dr. Kapoor reaches into the bowl and his grin is pure evil when he reads whatever is written on the slip of paper in his hands. I glance nervously at Riya, who doesn't seem to notice. She's too focused on the category itself, celebrating a small victory.

"Today, both teams will be completing the same challenge."

*The same challenge.* Sabotage could really, really screw things up in a direct, side-by-side dish comparison. But no. No, I'm not thinking about that. Not today. Today I am thinking about victory. At least this small one. Today I am focused.

"The dessert you will be making today is baked Alaska."

A ripple of terror goes through the kitchen.

"*Baked Alaska?*" I say through clenched teeth. "We don't have enough time!"

"That's the point," Tess hisses, lip curling.

Baked Alaska involves pound cake, a perfect meringue, and baking *ice cream* without melting it. (Or sometimes, just setting the thing on actual fire.) It's freaking impossible to make perfect in six hours, but in an *hour and a half*?

Now I'm panicking. But hey, we're *all* panicking, so it's fine. It's all fine.

Reid's team has nine people while we still have the full twelve, and the second the timer chimes out our start, I'm thinking maybe they actually have an advantage, because twelve is too many. We're scattering around like rats over here.

In a kitchen. I shudder at that mental image and sprint over to somewhere in the middle-ish of a dozen freaking out teenagers.

"OKAY," Andrew booms out, and I have to lend it to him, he does have a voice that carries. "I'll start on the pound cake, with . . ." He cocks his head, then points to Riya, some pretty, tall girl I don't know, and another cute, really small girl I also haven't really met. "You, you, and you."

"No," says Riya. I raise my eyebrows and Riya straightens, jaw hard.

"What?"

"Absolutely not. I'm not touching your damn pound cake, and you're not the head chef of this kitchen. We let you run it last challenge and the *only* reason three of us are still standing here is because Reid apparently sucks at walking, so no. No. I will not be joining you on the pound cake."

My eyes have got to be the size of a surprised anime character's—covering like a full three-quarters of my face. And there is complete, shocked silence.

Then a small kid who looks like he's *maybe* in the ninth grade says, "I got it," and joins the other two with Andrew.

"Desserts are what I do. I'm taking the ice cream machine. Two of you come with me."

Andrew furrows his big brow, still standing there just totally, deliciously stunned, and says, "Wouldn't it be easier to just use some ice cream from the freezer? We're short on time."

Riya tosses her head and walks off, laughing. "Yeah, I'm sure it would. Bet you a full ride scholarship that's an empty freezer, stud."

Riya does not slow down on the way to the ice cream machine, and three people (one more than she bargained for) scamper after her. She sends two back toward the pantry immediately, and I blink back at Andrew.

"I've got the meringue," I say. "Addie, you want to come with?"

"Yeah," she says.

The other two sprint back toward the pantry and in a few minutes, everything is running smoothly. I'm still not sure how freezing Riya's ice cream for presumably barely an hour is going to work out when we should have like *eight* to do this right, but they know. They know they screwed us on time. They want to see how we fix it.

I look around the kitchen, a flurry, then calm down.

We have a little time before we need to make the meringue; it's really Riya who needs to be freaking out. "I'm going to use the ice cream machine" is usually the death note for anyone on any cooking competition show, ever. But she is cool and collected, waiting while her ice cream churns, and like five people are hanging out with her now. I notice Andrew staring at the group with intense, unblinking, creeper eyes. He can't stand not being in charge today.

I smile, then watch as Riya takes her ice cream out and, miracle of miracles, at least from here, it looks perfect.

She tastes it quickly and the absolute sunshine on her face says it tastes perfect, too.

The other boy at the ice cream machines waits a little before he takes his out, and his sharp, "Shit, shit, shit, shit," can only indicate one thing: his ice cream is butter.

I do a tiny little fist pump in the air and wait out the ice cream's too minimal freezing time until the clock starts to tick down, and it's time to make the meringue.

One of the ingredient-fetchers scampers up to me while Addie cleans the beaters with a slice of lemon, and says, "I don't—I couldn't find the cream of tartar. It's kind of a mess back there but I swear it just isn't here—"

She doesn't have to finish her sentence. I cut one sharp look across the kitchen to see exactly who has it. Because he has a bowl and beaters and eggs and of course. *Of course* Reid is doing the meringue for his team.

I throw my shoulders back and try to look regal marching across the kitchen.

Reid has a mixing bowl in one hand and a teaspoon of white powder in the other. There's cream of tartar and a couple other boxes of stuff I don't care about open behind him.

I clear my throat.

Reid turns around and raises an eyebrow at me, leaning on his elbows against the counter.

"What d'you need, sugarplum?"

My nostrils flare at the nickname and I say, "That," cocking my head toward his left hand.

His eyes flick over to the teaspoon and then back down at me. He stands straight and tall, then takes a step toward me so there's hardly space between our chests.

Suddenly I'm shaking a little, and that's frustrating.

"You want this?" He holds out the teaspoon.

"Yes," I say. I'm not looking at the teaspoon; I'm looking at him.

I can feel the brush of his breath over my ear when he leans in and whispers, "Say please."

I clench my jaw. I can feel his cheek move when he smiles.

"Screw yourself."

"Rude," he says, but he's smirking when he hands me the teaspoon, which is way more than I actually need for the meringue.

My eyes are still burning into his when I snatch it from him. Well as much as someone can *snatch* something when they're trying like hell not to spill it. Then I get out of his side of the kitchen as fast as I can and practically throw the powder I need into the egg whites and sugar.

Time ticks down.

Addie has the stuff on as high a speed as she can manage and the meringue isn't coming together like I'm used to, which is stressful but we should have expected it. We whip and whip and whip, and I can feel the frustration bubbling up in my chest, filling every available space.

"What the hell?" I say. "Why aren't the peaks . . . peaking?"

"I do not know," says Addie, accent coming out stronger in her panic.

Finally, they start to form, not as strong as I'd like, but enough that we can make it work. This turned out not to be complete disaster.

Riya takes her ice cream out of the freezer and gets it on top of Andrew's pound cake, which is irritatingly pretty (I mean, it's a good thing. It's irritating because it's Andrew's), and we spread the meringue on top of it. The ice cream isn't as solid as it should be, but it also isn't butter, which has got to work in our favor, and they didn't give us eight hours. They had to have expected this.

The meringue goes on and it . . . doesn't look as gorgeous as my meringue usually does, but it's fine. It's pretty enough. We have less than a minute—no time to waste mourning, no time to taste anything; we barely have time to burn the top. Tess gets her hand on a blowtorch, which kind of seems like a bad idea to give us access to, and she lights the thing up.

The meringue is a little melty from that, but the lines are pretty and it's holding up well enough, and the brown running through the white meringue swirls is pretty damn delectable-looking, if I say so myself.

We cut slices and get the plates out with four seconds to spare.

I'm feeling good, proud standing in front of the judges today. Maybe Reid and I are in a truce, which would not be the worst thing. Tit for tat, the end.

We can go through the rest of this competition as respectful competitors, not archnemeses. The other team is praised widely for their presentation—four tiny baked Alaskas rather than one giant one in slices. It's adorable, and I wish I'd thought of it. A graham crackery thing on bottom instead of cake. They went with chocolate ice cream—bold, but the judges all seem to agree that though it's not correctly done, and it's a little odd, the buttery, slightly melty texture of their ice cream does go surprisingly well with the dark chocolate flavor. The technical flaw is points against them, but it could have been worse.

I smile over at Riya and she's beaming. Her ice cream is perfect. Frozen, barely melty at all inside, and sweet, perfectly textured strawberry. The judges take their bites. And every one of their faces instantly puckers. Down the line, like a terrible, heart-wringing version of The Wave.

My stomach drops into my feet.

The ice cream, and the cake—they're both hailed as perfect.

"The meringue, though," says Dr. Pearce. He just blinks, and something like electricity shoots down my spine.

Dr. Kapoor says, "I agree," and everyone takes another bite, just the meringue.

I look over at Addie, who throws her hands in the air in a shrug, and behind her, Andrew is staring daggers at me.

"It's . . . the texture is a bit odd, to be sure," says Dr. Lavell. "But the flavor is utterly bizarre."

"Vinegar," Dr. Freeman adds in a confident baritone, "was a . . . bold choice."

That's not possible. It's not.

"*Bold* is certainly a word for it," says Dr. Kapoor and the matter is settled. There is *vinegar* in the weird-textured meringue and it all goes *very* strangely with the strawberry and somehow, I, or Addie, or the other two who got us the ingredients . . .

We are dismissed, and I stand there for a full six seconds before I can build up the will to look at Reid. His mouth is tugging up.

Then I rush over to his station and pay attention to the boxes I ignored earlier. Graham, sugar, stuff someone used for the crust, I'm sure.

And open. White vinegar powder.

The teaspoon flashes through my mind. He wasn't going to use it; he was waiting for *me*.

Not just waiting for me to grab it mindlessly.

He told me to beg for it.

My eyes fly open, fury crashing over me like a storm. I catch his eye just as he leaves, and he grins with one corner of his mouth, then throws me a lazy, two-fingered salute.

He moves through the doorway and disappears.

# CHAPTER EIGHT

Andrew slams his shoulder into mine that night at dinner and my whole tray goes crashing to the ground. Spaghetti, garlic bread, one rogue meatball that has made its way across the whole dining hall to a table in the corner furthest from me. It's on the floor, it's on me. Freaking fantastic.

The hall falls silent after the clatter, and I just stare at Andrew, slack-jawed.

"Oh shit," he says, too slowly to be believable. "I'm so clumsy." He tosses me a single napkin and heads to his table with a few others from his team. Catty asshole.

Reid walks into the cafeteria about half a second later, and there I am, drowning in red and noodle, and my face is probably the same color as the sauce. He stops short and blinks. "Do you need—"

"Get the hell away from me," I hiss, and he purses his lips, then straightens and walks off to the line with the long, confident strides of a boy who is not, and does not foresee himself ever being, drenched in marinara.

"Will's picking up an extra plate for you," says Riya, crouching down next to me like it's nothing, like I haven't just been completely humiliated in front of every freaking person here, like when I stand, my shoes don't squeak and slip against the sauce on the floor. She picks me up by the arm and I take my tray. We move together, allies, to the trash can where I dump everything, and then I follow her, nose in the air like I am a damn sixteenth-century monarch, to our table.

"Red's your color," says Will the second I sit, and my eyebrows jump up. There's a half-second of silence, and I can feel Riya tense beside me, and then a laugh just bubbles out of me.

"You asshole," I say.

"Asshole who brought you some non-floor-contaminated spaghetti and garlic bread, thank me very much."

"Thank you very much," I say, and he smirks and takes a bite of his pasta.

Riya says, "It could have happened to anyone."

"This disaster or the kitchen white vinegar powder disaster?"

"Both."

I blow out a breath. And eat.

And feel everyone's eyes on me like a tangible thing, whether or not it's real.

I chew and swallow mechanically, the smell of oregano and basil and garlic soaking into my skin, until I just can't. I just can't stay here for one more second.

I leave the table without saying a word to Riya or Will and practically run to my room.

I miss everyone. Back at home—Mom and Dad and Jillian and Em and everyone who is not *here*. Everyone who sees me as more than a tool to help them win or a competitor for them to beat.

I slam my door and strip out of my shirt and pull on this too-big cheap Star Wars *Keep it, it suits you* shirt that Jillian got me one Christmas. And I can feel myself just begin to relax.

It smells like home.

Mom and Dad are both working, and Em is working and probably trying to seduce Pool Girl at the same time, but Jillian works online while she's home on break.

I pray she'll answer.

"Hey, baby sister," she says on the first ring.

And what I say is: "Hrggghhh." Which is what happens when you open your mouth and start to form words but start sobbing instead.

"So I guess I shouldn't ask how things are going?"

I gasp. And I'm so annoyed that all these jerks can affect me like this. That they have me doing that gulping crying thing I haven't done since I got stood up at homecoming in the tenth grade, and Em had to step in and be my date.

"I'm okay," I say.

"That's what I was gonna guess, yeah."

"God, Jillian, everyone here is just. Mean. They're mean. I don't know how else to say it or how to fix it but I miss you."

"You miss *me*? Damn, things must really be shitty over there."

She says it in this teasing tone that I can picture coming with a flick to my nose. Jillian and I have had our share of fights over the years, but we've always been each other's favorites.

"I miss you too, Bug," she says.

"Yeah?"

"Well, I miss your cooking. We're slowly wasting away over here in House Lane."

I laugh. It comes out a little watery but it's a real laugh. "Jerk."

"Of course."

"Does it make me a little kid to say I think I'm just . . . sad? To be away from home?"

"Nah, it makes you sound like a college freshman."

I smile.

"Listen," says Jillian, "I've been brushing up on my muay thai so if you need me to come kick some little chef asses, I will, but until I can get there, why don't you turn on *Mean Girls*? I'll turn it on at the same time."

"You wanna watch a movie with me? When I should be socializing?" I roll my eyes even though she can't see it and say in fake exasperation, "Ugh, she doesn't even *go* here."

And Jillian says, "God, have you found it yet? I'm old. Or getting there."

I giggle and swipe through streaming apps until I find one that has it, thank everything.

We click play at the same time.

It's past ten when I follow Riya and Addie out back. We don't have to be in our rooms until midnight, and even that is a completely lax rule that I don't think anyone follows. We haven't experienced a single bed check, and I hear doors opening and closing down the hall at all times. So no one is really counting.

There's this little area outside by a creek, because I think every single place is by some kind of creek in Georgia, and apparently we're hanging out there. Will is the only guy from the other team here. It strikes me as odd, then, that we've cordoned ourselves off from each other because of these random group assignments. But we have. When I walk up, arms linked with Riya, Andrew glances at me and his face darkens.

"So damn glad you could make it," he says.

I narrow my eyes. "You've made that clear, dude."

"Have I?"

I stay standing, even though Andrew is on the ground, leaning back against a tree. Like I need this massive height difference to hold my own. Like we are gearing up for a fight. "It was one mistake."

"That's going to screw us."

"You don't know that," I say.

And once again, the whole freaking group is quiet, listening to Andrew rip me apart. Or try. I feel so tiny, and like I want to be tall. But I don't know how to be. Andrew knows, down in the pit of his stomach, that I don't deserve to be here.

Maybe he's right. I don't know. I *did* screw up.

I want to disappear down into the ground. My gut twists traitorously in sympathy for Reid. This is what he felt like the other night. Because of me.

But his shittiness is what is causing me to feel this way, right now. So the sympathy dissipates pretty damn quickly, little mental effort required.

Andrew's mouth twists into something cruel and he takes a cigarette he smuggled in here from his pocket and lights it. "I'm just saying, next challenge, maybe try not being such a dumbass. We're all paying for it, and I'm gonna be pissed if it's not you paying."

Suddenly all the shame just snaps and gives way to rage. "*I'm* the dumbass?" I say, skin hot and eyes wide. "The first challenge, if Reid hadn't tripped and spilled their dessert, *you* would have sent three of us home because you're too stupid to know how to cook scallops."

"Who's Reid?"

I blink. And that's when Will slides close to me and says, overenunciating and slow, "The guy who tripped. And spilled their dessert."

Andrew sucks in on his cigarette and stands, then blows it right in my face. I cough, and I'm mad about it. Like the satisfaction he gets out of my coughing is the most offensive thing happening right now. "I don't need to stand here and take this," says Andrew, and when he leaves, it's nothing but crickets in the air for a while. Crickets and a creek and six kids just kind of breathing in the dark.

Until Riya says, "Where's everyone from?" and the tension mercifully cracks.

I don't even know Riya, really. And I know Will even less. But I am basically clinging to both of them like they're handholds on a rock wall, because even with Andrew gone, no one will quite look at me. I think they wouldn't have cared so much, except he set the bar. Made me a target. And that has basically made it so that anything less than tripping me in the cafeteria and berating me in front of everyone is considered mercy.

So I just chill beside Riya, who keeps jerking into me and giggling because Will keeps poking her in the side and winking at her, and I ignore the chill in the air that I'm sure is actually warm. Because it's Savannah in June.

When it finally tips past midnight, we go inside and I fall asleep going over and over what I can do to get vengeance on Reid.

# CHAPTER NINE

This week, the individual dish is a low-key thing. No sprinting around or grabbing for ingredients in a mad dash of flour and milk and paprika. It's just "be a chef. Cook good food. Take less than two hours. The end." Which is exactly what I needed. To relax into the exquisite deglazing of a sauté pan and be able to appreciate the heat that blows out of the oven when I open it, not view it as a health hazard when someone yanks it open as I sprint past it.

We *all* needed this.

I was so glad for the moment to breathe that I didn't even give a second thought to sabotaging Reid. Not that it would have mattered; everyone knew our team would be the one losing members, not his.

Three members of my team left after the individual challenge ended. Not Riya or Addie, thank goodness. Not Andrew, either, because someone up there hates me.

That puts us at eighteen chefs. Teams are even. And I am well-rested enough from the simple challenge this week that now I can focus my energy back where it naturally wants to go: getting vengeance on Reid.

I am walking the campus in the early morning fog, pondering. Tar and feather, quartering, burning all of his pants if I can find a way into his room—a number of creative solutions—when there's a shadow beside me and a thumping on the pavement. Rhythmic puffs of breath that sound vaguely masculine. I turn.

Reid is bouncing on his feet, a thick ring of sweat darkening the neckline of his shirt. He has headphones in but he pops one out to say, "Hey there, buttercup." He smiles. A genuine smile. I can feel my fist curling at my side.

"Reid."

"Early morning communion with nature?"

He's still bouncing, warding off that lactic acid with movement, so all his words come out short and off-pitch and wrong. "Not exactly," I say.

I have stopped walking, apparently. I cross my arms over my chest. "What are *you* doing?"

He raises a single eyebrow and gestures to his entire self, hand quickly drawing my eyes to his damp face, his torso, his hips, down to his legs, which are frustratingly beautiful things. Like God assigned the sculpting of Reid Yamada's calves to Michelangelo, and Michelangelo approached them with the goal of rendering *David* a piece of shit. I blink hard to clear that thought. "What's it look like I'm doing?"

"Sullying a perfectly beautiful morning with chatter? And—oh my gosh, will you please stop the bouncing? I can barely hear what you're saying."

He rolls his eyes but stands still. After he's been immobile for more than half a second, he bends over and rests his hands on his knees, breathing hard. His shirt is super loose, with those excessively deep athletic dude armholes, so when he does, they gap hard and I can see everything— his collarbone and stomach and . . . good lord, what a perfect chest.

I bite my tongue and look away. Then say, primly, while looking across the courtyard, "Who runs this early in the morning?"

"You think I should run at three in the afternoon? When it's eight hundred degrees out and the air itself is a swamp?"

"Well," I say.

"Well." He cocks his head. "And who communes with nature at such an ungodly hour?"

"I told you. I wasn't communing."

He's standing tall again, one hand in his hair, the other relaxed at his side. "Then what were you doing?"

"I don't have to tell you."

He laughs, this big, loud, shockingly genuine thing, and I'm kind of startled by it. I know I sound like a little kid. Petulant. *I don't have to tell you.* But I don't want to talk to him, not after the hell of last week, not after he started all of this in the first place. I want to not-commune with nature far away from here. Where his cocky smirk is not invading my peripheral and the smell of deodorant and sweat isn't completely consuming my ability to form coherent words.

"You ready for the personal challenge tomorrow?" he says.

I blow out a breath of laughter. "Yeah. You're not screwing me this time, Yamada. I'm done."

"Oh?" Reid's frustratingly perfect flop of hair finds its way down over his eyes. "You want to call a truce?"

I narrow my eyes. "Not on your life."

He sticks a single earbud back in his ear and bites his lip when he smiles. "I'm *breathless* with anticipation, princess." And he runs off, tennis shoes thump-thump-thumping on the pavement.

My shoulders drop when he's almost out of sight, and I didn't realize until now that my muscles were tense, on edge, through our entire conversation. I purse my lips. I have honestly no idea what I'm going to do to him tomorrow except whatever it is, he's going to expect it. I won't be able to hand him the wrong ingredient or knock into him so he falls or sabotage something he's mixing; he's going to be ready and alert. Which means I have to think.

I feel kind of bad even pondering it. But he was the one who couldn't let it lie, couldn't just call it even. He asked for me to retaliate then, and he's basically literally begging me for it now. I am not interested in guilt.

I'm *not*.

I'm interested in revenge.

I look up at the sky, hoping for a magical answer to appear in the clouds. And when none does, I resign myself to walking back to the old culinary building. It's long and slow; I must have walked farther than I planned. Mist is curling around my ankles; it looks apocalyptic almost. The whole way back, I contemplate vengeance and cooking and evil smirks and floppy hair.

"Save me from this nightmare, Em," I say into the phone. There is a dramatic sigh on the other end.

"Tell me your struggles, babe."

I flop back onto my bed, muscles unwinding. I can actually feel it—this is the first second I haven't been stressed since I got here. "Tell me yours first."

"If you insist." I can hear Em smiling through the phone; she has a particularly smiley smile-voice. "So I told you Sophie was coming over again? After several very platonic coming-overs. Well she did and we turned on *Top Gun*, which is the gayest straight movie of all time."

I bark out a laugh. "No one watches *Top Gun* anymore."

"Well," she says, "neither did we."

It takes me a second, then I pump my fist in the air. "FINALLY."

"Fiiiiiinallyyyy."

I laugh and say, "Have you guys hung out since?"

"A lady doesn't kiss and tell, Carter."

"You already told."

"Then yes. We have. We have *not watched Top Gun* like eight times; it's turning into a hell of a summer."

"I have not *not watched Top Gun* with anyone at this college, which is a real tragedy."

"Get your shit together then."

I groan. "I can't. I don't have time."

"For getting your shit together or for making out?"

"Either one."

There is a short pause, and then, "Well then what are you using that time on?"

I sigh. "Studying. Watching cooking shows. Plotting the downfall of one Reid Yamada. Stop raising your eyebrow."

"I wasn't raising my eyebrow."

"Yes, you were."

She laughs.

"There's nothing eyebrow-raisey about it," I say. "He's just this guy here who went out of his way to completely screw me on day one. And now things have, like, escalated. I'm out of ways to life-ruin and I need to ruin his life."

"How did he screw you?"

"In the kitchen," I say. Then immediately. "DON'T. DO NOT."

Em snorts and says, "You are asking way too much of me here." There is a pause, charged with Em's valiant attempt to say nothing, but then she says, in obvious sharp relief, "A bedroom would be a more obvious place, though."

And then my brain lights up. *Bedroom.*

"Em," I say. I glance at my clock. It's getting dark and mostly everyone is out and about, taking advantage of nighttime. Half of them are down by the creek, playing in the water like kids. Riya asked me to come and I declined, on account of desperately needing some no-physical-contact-with-humans time. "I have to go."

"Whattttt? No! I haven't talked to you since you left."

"Just . . ." I say. "Listen. Let me call you back in a few minutes. I have to do a thing."

"Ugh, fine," she says, and I end the call, then slide my phone back into my sweatpants.

I crack open my door and glance down the hall, like leaving my room is the nerve-wracking thing. Then I open it when it becomes clear that it's empty. And then it's clear to me that everyone could be outside my room right now and no one would care that I am leaving it.

I walk down the hall until I have officially crossed from the girls' side to the boys' side and everything feels too quiet, too easy, too . . . lord, what am I doing?

I reach Reid's room, or what I assume is his room, since I've seen him heading into it a few times at night, and take a breath. Knock. Softly, so no one hears it and thinks it's for them. My stomach twists—I know it's just him in there; his roomie got knocked out the first night, but I am realizing now that if he *is* in there, I have no story at all about what has brought me here to knock on his door at night.

My face is bright red, I bet. I can feel it. It's so hot I think if I touched it I would burn my fingers. But mercifully, after a few seconds, no one answers.

So I square my shoulders, and push the door open, then close it behind me.

It smells like Reid in here. I hadn't noticed he had a particular smell, but people's living spaces always wind up smelling like them, I think. It's not amazing or terrible; it mostly smells like butter and the spicy body wash he must have pretty recently used and like . . . like someone who spends a lot of time in a kitchen. I'm rising up on my tiptoes apparently, tightness all the way down to the soles in my feet. I force myself back down to the flats and all the tension that left my body talking to Em has just magically reappeared. As I suspected, Reid is extremely the source of it.

It's kind of messy in here, Reid's bed only halfway made, a bunch of crap all strewn over his former roommate's bed. His T-shirt from this morning is crumpled on the floor. When I see it, my throat practically closes up and suddenly I feel very guilty being here.

I am *wracked* with it, out of nowhere, crawling up my throat and pinching at my stomach. Like this is a violation. It kind of is, honestly.

I look at the door—I could leave. I should. I should go. This is really not cool—but then I see it. There like a shining beacon of temptation.

*Destroy me, Carter. Destroy meeee.*

His phone.

He's got to be down with everyone at the creek and didn't want to get it wet. And this was the plan, but I was half-assing it honestly. Was planning on screwing up the alarm on the clock by his bedside table and just crossing my fingers he had relied only on that for a wakeup. But this? This is a sign.

I have no choice.

I switch the alarm on his nightstand first, from a.m. to p.m. Tomorrow is an early-morning challenge and I'm willing to bet he won't wake up on his own without an alarm.

My hands are shaking when I go for his phone.

It's a violation, it's *such* a damn violation.

But he doesn't even have a freaking passcode on here. Who doesn't have a passcode on their phone?

I navigate to Clock, and yup. He has an alarm set for 5:30 a.m.

My thumb hovers over it.

Knots and flip-flops in my stomach.

*I am breathless with anticipation, princess.*

I click p.m.

Then I sprint the hell out of his room and practically rocket down the hall into my own bed.

# CHAPTER TEN

I am sweating throughout the entire individual challenge. It's early enough in the morning that everyone is about half asleep, or we were when we got here. My hair is a wreck, and several kids still smell like the creek, and it's all just a mess in here.

A mess that is short one person.

We had an hour today, another time-lenient challenge, to create something small and beautiful and extravagant, which makes anything anyone will make just impossibly annoying on principle. Basically the Tiny Houses of food.

There is a half-hour left, and my merlot is reducing on the stove, sweetness and pungency bubbling up in the air. I pull out a knife to start slicing my duck, stomach twisting. Reid isn't here yet. Thirty minutes late and I wonder if the judges have noticed or if there are so many of us, they won't realize until judging comes up and his name isn't there.

I feel annoyingly guilty. Man, I hate having a conscience; life would be so much simpler if we could just be done with them altogether when we needed to be. But that is not real, and so I am assailed with it.

I am halfway through slicing this duck breast when the door to the kitchen slams opens and in runs Reid. He's red-faced, hair completely wild, the part that isn't shaved smushed up on one side. He's wearing Deadpool pajamas and these beat-up tennis shoes and he looks absolutely panicked.

"What's the challenge, what are we doing?" I hear him whisper frantically to Will, who looks like he hasn't got a lot to do; whatever he's making won't take him the full hour.

Will leans over to tell him in this low voice and Reid just hisses, "Shit. Shit shit." He jerks an apron over himself and runs his hand violently over the tuft on top of his head. He knots the rope aggressively, like it has done him a personal offense. I whirl away from him and focus on my own stuff. I can't afford to be derailed by him, not again. And he's not giving a second thought to me. I slice.

Prepare my pan with butter and saffron, a pinch of garlic. There's only twenty minutes left and Reid is swearing up a storm somewhere, clanging around. I glance up when I reach for a few herbs and start chopping, and see the judges glancing at each other, looking down their noses. They keep looking over at Reid, and oh man, he is in such deep shit.

He doesn't seem to notice, he's so focused on making up forty minutes of lost time.

I get my duck in the pan, stir my merlot, prepare the little veggie and crostini base of the appetizer, and when it's perfectly pink inside, I take it off the burner. It smells totally divine. It *tastes* totally divine. The wine sauce is utterly absurd, it's so incredible. I never get to cook duck at home, so I'm dying to just eat the whole thing myself and straight up drink the spiced butter out of the sauté pan.

I'm wrapping ingredients, arranging them on the plates, drizzling reductions in perfect patterns, and I have enough extra time to make up more than four. I wind up with six completed plates when time is called, and the prettiest four are set up front. I cut a glance over at Reid's. He looks relaxed, like he can breathe. Hands in the pockets of his apron and slouching a little. He's still kind of a wreck, *covered* in purple sauce and flour and who knows what else, but that easy expression is back on his face, in the rest of his muscles. I have no idea what on earth his dish is, but there's some kind of green vegetable, zucchini probably, that's all thin like a noodle and curling up around some kind of red meat in a sauce, and suddenly I am mad.

He had twenty minutes, and he made *that*.

I glance down at my dishes, which seem inadequate now. Not because they suck, but because I'm hearing *Reid Yamada made this in twenty minutes! With a box of scraps!* And his is so beautiful it's like my covert ops last night did nothing at all.

He catches my eye from across the kitchen and winks at me. I feel it in my toes.

I face forward, and we present our dishes to the judges, one by one. After we go down the line, we are dismissed, because of the infuriating rule that says until the competitor numbers sink, we can't be judged then and there personally.

After we are free to leave, I pick up one of my little duck creations on a spare plate and eat it. So much tender loving care, so much good butter and wine spent, it feels like a crime to let it all go to waste. I shut my eyes for a second and the crisp duck skin, the velvet bitter-sweet of the wine, that hint of saffron, a little basil, takes me over. I love this moment. I love *food*.

Food like this. That I never, ever get to indulge in at home except through a television screen, and every great once in a while, when my home-ec teacher lets me go nuts in the kitchen.

"Proud of yourself?" says Reid when he passes me.

"Yes, I am," I say. The kitchen is still a whir of activity and everyone leaving, so I can get away with this, I think. With this conversation and eating my own food.

"Is that duck?" he says, and it's like he's not even mad. He's . . . chipper, even.

"It is."

"Can I try one?"

I'm so taken aback by his use of human manners that I say, "Go for it."

*Why aren't you furious at me? Halfway to murder? What is happening?*

He pops one in his mouth and I can see that instant change in his face that says it's good—a flash of a look that people can't fake. Then he schools his expression into a warm neutral.

"Well?" I say. The room is clearing out so I move for the door.

Reid says, smiling, "Not bad." Then he winks at me again and leaves.

Riya is waiting for me outside the kitchen, frowning at Reid when he passes her. "He's going to get eliminated."

"I don't know." It comes out sounding completely robotic. Like I am an actual android tasked with never displaying human emotion, even under duress.

Riya furrows her brow. "He completely wrecked his team's dessert and then he gets shown mercy and shows up *forty minutes late* to a challenge this morning? Honestly, why is he even here if he doesn't care about it?"

I shrug, swallow hard. "I'm sure he cares about it."

"I thought we hated Reid Yamada."

I scrape my teeth over my lip. "We do," I say, and we walk back toward the dorm.

It's like seven p.m., just after dinner, when I hear voices coming from the other side of the common room. One of them is sharp and feminine, and the other is definitely Reid's.

I am walking in the opposite direction, toward my bedroom. I have an epic night of Netflix and literally nothing else at all planned and I have been looking forward to it all day, but that sharp voice is going all in, and I think I hear Reid stuttering. I have to turn around.

I'm quiet, walking through the common room, feet padding softly on the ancient-looking rug on the floor, and I stop by the fireplace. It's lit, like I think it always is, and the light crackles will camouflage the sound of my breathing, I think. I shrink against the wall just outside the hall.

"It's unacceptable, Mr. Yamada."

"I know, I—"

"Do you?" It's Dr. Lavell. I recognize her voice now. "Do you understand how exactly you're coming off here? After the disaster the first week—"

"I swear that was not my fault. I—"

"Do *not* interrupt me, Mr. Yamada."

There's this charged silence. Then a quiet, legitimately humble, "Yes ma'am."

"After the disaster the first week, we thought you would take this seriously. As seriously as someone who's been given a second chance in a program where even the first was a significant privilege. But showing up halfway through a challenge like that is a serious problem. It shows a lack of discipline, of dedication, of passion, and I am nearly inclined to send you packing right now."

"Dr. Lavell, *please*." His voice cracks and there is that throat-crushing guilt again. This is not as fun a game as I had thought it would be, maybe. Stupid conscience, ruining everything. "I swear I want this more than anything."

"Do you?" Her voice is Alan Rickman–level nonplussed.

"It was my alarm, and I know that's a bullsh—terrible excuse. I know. I'm an idiot and I should have double-checked a.m. or p.m.. Trust me when I say I have spent the last fourteen hours doing nothing but regret this. But I want this so bad I can taste it. And I'm a good chef, I know I'm a good chef. And I'm so, so sorry. I swear if you give me another chance, I'll prove it to you."

His voice is so sincere, and I am digging my fingers into the wall, clenching my jaw until it hurts.

I hear her answer as they're leaving the hall, and my only hope of avoiding detection is to shrink back into this wall until I disappear. She says, "Very well. But one more misstep and I will throw you out of this program so fast your head will spin, young man."

"Yes ma'am. Thank you, ma'am."

Dr. Lavell doesn't see me. I'm breaking into a cold sweat hoping Reid won't either when he says, without looking at me, "Hey, trouble."

"Who, me?" I say, stepping out of the corner and smirking with a confidence I absolutely do not feel.

Reid does this almost-laugh and looks over at me, scratching his chest. "I'm so screwed," he says. His voice is thin and drawn and frustrated. Sad, almost, which makes me wildly uncomfortable.

"So I heard."

"Your mother never taught you not to eavesdrop?" He faces me finally, raising his eyebrow.

"I'm sure she did."

"Rebel scum," he says, and I laugh.

There's this feeling in my chest, light, like there are little bubbles in it, like I'm going to just lift off the floor, while at the same time I want to burrow down into its depths.

"This one isn't even your fault. The irony." He furrows his brow. "It's not really ironic, I guess. Just bullshit. Ha."

A sweat breaks out at my hairline. "Yep. Ha. Not ironic, though, that's an improper use of that word, but you know. Mistakes. And all." *Stop babbling, oh god, stop.*

He narrows his eyes. "You okay there?"

"Me? Fine."

"You're looking a little . . ."

"Tired?"

"Nervous," he says. His voice rings with finality and something zings in my throat. He takes a step toward me and I would step backward except I'm already standing in the corner, and there is nowhere for me to go. I cross my arms over my chest.

"I don't know where you're getting that," I say. It's hard to swallow.

"I set two alarms for today," he says. "My phone *and* my actual clock."

I shrug.

"Holy shit," he says. He takes another step forward, and I can see the vein pulsing in his neck, the set of his jaw. He looks me up and down, appraising. *Evaluating.* Then comes to his conclusion. "It was you?"

When he inhales, his chest expands, and we're standing so close, I'm surprised it doesn't brush against my arms. I breathe.

I'm not actually scared of him, there's nothing about him that really freaks me out. But I am scared of getting caught. Because, dammit, I crossed a line. There was a line that neither of us had talked about and I knew I was crossing it while I was doing it, and . . . shit. Shit shit.

"Back off," I say.

He immediately puts his hands in the air and takes a step back. I could leave if I wanted.

"Say it," he says, hands still in the air.

I meet his eyes, and now I'm defiant. That's the only thing I can feel, even though what he is accusing me of is entirely true. "Say what?" I speak spite, I think, more fluently than English.

"Carter. Admit that you did it."

"I don't—"

"Carter—Jesus. Just—"

"Fine!" I say, and my voice is louder than I thought it would be. "I did."

He drops his hands. "You *snuck* into my *room*? You were in my room."

"Listen—"

"No. You listen. Every person here knows that would be bullshit. Going into my room without my permission, going through my cell phone, like, in what world is that okay?"

"You started this, Reid."

His voice slices like a knife when he says, "Okay, then FINISH IT."

I blink.

"I almost got kicked out of the program, do you get that?" He looks up at the ceiling, blows out a breath. "I. Am. Sorry. I'm sorry. I'm sorry I screwed you over that first day; how many *fucking times* do I need to say it? IIII. AAMMM. SORRRRRYYYY."

Shame is burning me up from the inside, curling my stomach like paper on fire.

"I told you I would get you back."

"Yeah, but I didn't think it would mean you going through my *shit*, Carter. That's not a proportional response to me switching out cream of tartar for white vinegar powder."

"That's the nature of revenge."

He looks down at me, backs up a couple steps. "Okay."

I frown. "Okay?"

"Yeah," he says. He shrugs and looks over my shoulder at the wall instead of me. Then he just says, "Have a good rest of your day." And leaves.

# CHAPTER ELEVEN

One from each team goes home after the tiny plate challenge. Reid is in the bottom four again, but everyone knows it was the lateness that did it, and he must be an *incredible* chef because whatever he is making keeps pulling him through, even though the judges obviously want to send him home.

There are sixteen of us left, eight on each team, and tonight everyone is hanging out just off campus, by the actual river. It's this roaring thing, not at all like the creek, and if this was not a teacher-sanctioned event, I would be very concerned there would be alcohol, which would prompt me to be very concerned that someone would fall into the river and never be heard from again.

But the program heads are here, and even they are all just having soda. There's food laid out on the table—not gourmet food. Hot dogs and southern potato salad, and like three different types of barbeque. I didn't even know there *were* three different types of barbeque. It's refreshing, honestly.

Everyone is just . . . relaxed. Addie is flirting with this cute freckled girl in pigtails, and cute freckled girl is laughing pretty hard, which is probably a good sign.

Will keeps acting like he's going to jump in the river, which keeps prompting Riya to scream, to which he responds, "Riya, this is a classy event. Please try to keep your voice down." At one point, she tries to hit him for it and he catches her by the wrist and smiles, and she blushes so hard I think *she* might need to be thrown into the river to cool down.

They are so obviously "just friends" that it's painful.

"I'm trying to keep you alive, William."

He doesn't let go of her wrist. "Dooooon't."

She drops her hand slowly, and it looks intentional. Like if she goes slow enough, he won't have an excuse to let go. He doesn't. "Don't what?"

"William is the worst name."

"I heard that!" yells some kid whose name actually *is* William (Will's is not) and they both jump, and Will drops her wrist immediately.

"Eavesdropping *again*," says Reid in my ear, and then I jump harder than either Riya or Will did. We haven't spoken in two days. Since he left me standing there alone in the common room, choking on guilt. He *tsks* and I roll my eyes.

"It's not eavesdropping if everyone can hear it."

"Oh, is that the rule?"

"What do you want?" I say.

"To accept your apology."

My mouth actually falls open and I turn to face him. "What did you say?"

"You know what I said."

I scoff. "Lord, you're intolerable."

"Let's have it, plum cake."

I roll my eyes. "Plum cake. You are reaching, my friend."

"Not until you apologize."

"What?"

"You can call me friend," he says, biting into an apple—a Red Delicious, which is just objectively a terrible choice, "after you apologize. Also it's not reaching; your hair is purple."

I fold my arms over my chest again, which is not a gesture I usually make that often but I find myself doing *a lot* of it lately. Reid, the common denominator. "It's reaching because it's not a nickname."

"Well." He smiles and my heart flip-flops. Curse it! "It is now."

He starts off toward the riverbank, and I grab a sweet tea that lives up to its name, and I guess I follow him.

The sun is starting to fall, and back in Montana that would mean putting on a jacket no matter what season it was, but in Savannah, it just means it gets darker. I'm out here in shorts and a little red tank top and I'm not even beginning to feel cold. It's warm and humid, moisture all in my skin and in my mouth when I breathe.

The crickets are out, too, but they're hard to hear over the river. Reid sits right there on the wet grass and I sit, too, and pick up a rock and toss it down to the flowing water below. It's farther off than it looks, and my rock hits dirt. Reid picks one up, too. His makes it. But barely.

"I'm sorry," I say.

He looks over at me, and I pick up a heavy rock from my left, then hurl it as hard as I can. It lands with a splash farther out than his did.

"Bravo," he says. Then he watches the water.

"I took it too far, okay?" I can't look at him because even here, just sitting throwing rocks into a river, he makes my blood boil. I still get mad that he started all of this for legitimately no reason, whether or not my retribution has been arguably a lot worse. And I don't want to see the satisfaction on his face when he gets this apology, but I have to give it. Because it sucks that he's not wrong . . . but he's not wrong. "I should have . . . I shouldn't have gone into your room without your permission."

"As though there is a scenario in which I would have given it," he says.

I can't tell if he's smiling but I don't look to see. If I take my eyes off the river, I won't get this apology out. I'm choking on it as it is. "I'm not sorry I screwed you over. I'm sorry about how I did it though."

It's quiet for so long that I have to turn and look at him.

He's looking at me. Like he's contemplating. "Okay," he says.

"Okay, what?"

"I said I came here to accept your apology, short stuff, and that is what I am doing."

"Okay," I say.

I look back over his shoulder and see Riya glancing our way. Will and Addie look over here, too, and I'm about to get up and leave to shut down the chance of any kind of weird speculation that I am *not* here for when Reid says, "Just so we're clear, I still hate you a lot."

I'm so surprised by it that I actually snort-laugh. He just raises his eyebrows and I say, "Well. The sentiment is mutual." He's rolling another little rock around in his fingers, not saying much, so I say, "In fact, I usually fall asleep thinking about punching you in the face."

He looks at me out of the corner of his eye and makes a (pretty impressive) throw. "How convenient. As I wake up thinking about wrapping my hands around your throat." He side-eyes me, deadpan. "Not hard enough to actually *kill* you."

"Thank you for your restraint."

"Well, I'm not a monster."

The fireflies are coming out now, lighting up the grass. Under any other circumstance, it would be unbearably romantic. I am doubly annoyed now.

Reid stands, brushes off his pants, and doesn't help me up, which is good because I would have spat on his hand. I stand and say, "I've considered just suffocating you with your pillow, Reid."

He says, "How rude. At least pick a quick or creative murder method. I can't abide one that's neither."

"You really are insufferable."

We are walking back to the picnic now. "Thank you. That means a lot coming from you. Moriarty to my Sherlock."

"I mean it sincerely. Brutus to my Caesar."

He laughs. "High-brow. Vader to my Skywalker."

"Technically, Vader is a Skywalker."

"Ugh, spoilers," he says.

"You are the Zuko to my Katara."

He stops, raises an eyebrow. "Oh? Well. That changes the dynamic, doesn't it?"

My mouth clamps shut of its own volition. "I always shipped Katara and Aang." (It's a lie. No one ships Katara and Aang. Zuko and Katara are the greatest rivals to what should have been lovers of all time.)

He narrows his eyes. "That. Is bullshit."

I stand my ground.

He just kind of laughs, then turns around. Ostensibly to head back toward the barbecue.

"So this hatchet," I say, and he looks back at me over his shoulder. "We calling it buried? Or?"

He barks out a laugh. Then laughs harder. And he keeps right on laughing until he disappears into the crowd.

I am . . . I am taking it as a no.

# CHAPTER TWELVE

I get back from the river after everyone else.

Well, I get back the *second* time later than everyone else. At some point, I apparently lost my phone and I've been frantically looking for it ever since. It's of course not a freaking iPhone so I can't just track the thing like everyone keeps telling me to do. I've spent three hours going back and forth between my room and the river, until now, when it's too dark.

I'm beginning to think some possum ate it or something, which is fantastic. I definitely can't afford to just buy a new one.

It was high-key stressing me out all night, and now here I am, hanging out with Riya and Addie, and the liquor Addie managed to snag from the store across the street that doesn't card has made it so I'm only low-key stressing over it now.

I am distracted by these girls, and actual, non-competitive, non-asshole-boys-related fun. It's past lights out, but at this point, lights out has gone from lax to nonexistent, so no one cares. Will could be in here, and he and Riya could have just like . . . hung a sock on the door and I bet no teacher would stop them. We're all high school juniors, but the staff here is extremely used to college kids. Not high schoolers who everyone else seems to think need supervision.

I have procured cookies to go with Addie's liquor. Crumbs are all over Riya's bed. (She had to give hers up to the cause since she didn't provide snacks. A fair sacrifice, I feel, but then I won't be the one sleeping on crumbs and chocolate chips all night.)

"So Carter."

"So Addie."

"You were sitting mighty close with your mortal enemy this evening."

I sniff and take a bite of the cookie, which is half the size of my face. "Oh, was I?"

She raises her eyebrow and Riya just smirks. Riya says, "I believe I even overheard something about you falling asleep thinking about him."

My face is so hot suddenly it surprises me, and I bite my tongue when I'm going for the cookie. "Shit," I say. You never realize how fast you move until you bump your head on something or how hard you bite until you injure your mouth.

"Geez, forget I asked," says Riya.

"No, no. My tongue." I'm lisping it and everyone is laughing.

Addie, however, will not be deterred. "Falling asleep thinking about him?"

"About *punching him*, Addie, that's different."

Her eyes are sparkling when she opens her mouth to speak so I cut her off. "You were standing *mighty close* to that cute little redhead, so I don't want to hear about it."

Addie laughs. "Yes," she says. "Because I want to make out with her."

"Well."

She shrugs.

Riya says, "She has a poin—"

"Oh no," I say, and I'm not sure why I feel, like, actually mad. "You and Will are so all over each other none of us can exist in the same space as you without getting lust all over us."

"What?" She shrieks it, like actually shrieks.

I look over at Addie, who locks glances with me, and we both look back at Riya. She's dark red and blinking. A lot.

Addie says, "Come on."

"We're friends."

I laugh, "Okay."

"I'm serious! We are. We're . . . friends."

I grin. "I, for one, spend all my time with my platonic friends poking them in the side and giggling and grabbing their wrists."

Riya purses her lips. "Will is touchy. I'm touchy."

Addie says, "Well, you've never grabbed *me* by the wrist."

"I didn't grab Will by the wrist!"

I'm laughing hard now that the conversation has turned from me and Reid to someone else, and then there is a knock on the door.

My grin goes a little wicked, and I say, "Probably your knight in shining armor right now," to Riya.

Riya hisses, "Carter—" and I open the door, laughing. Then freeze.

"You dropped this."

"Uh."

Reid is standing there in sweatpants and a black T-shirt, holding out my phone. I don't even have the mental wherewithal to fully process the relief. Because I am suddenly extremely aware of the full-on coat of crumbs on my own shirt, my pants. I lick a small piece of chocolate off the corner of my mouth and Reid's eyes flick down to it, then back to my eyes.

"You want it?" he says.

I blink and tell myself to stop thinking about how short these night shorts are and how giant this T-shirt is, then I just grab the hem so it's clear I'm wearing pants. "Yeah," I say. "Yeah, uh, thanks."

"Any time," he says. His eyes are dark and focused, and maybe it's just the lighting. Maybe it's the fact that they keep dipping down to my legs.

There's this awkward silence, then he says, in this quiet, almost deadpan voice, "Are you planning on taking it or?"

I bet I look like a beet. I bet beets would look at me and say, "Wow, that girl is red."

"Of course. Ha. Duh. I'm tired."

"Yeah?" he says. He cocks his head just the slightest bit, and the corner of his mouth cocks with it.

I snatch the phone back. "How did you get this?"

"It fell out of your pocket back at the river."

"You walked away before I did."

He smiles, teeth this dazzling straight white. "It fell out as soon as you sat down."

"I've been calling it all night." He says nothing, just keeps right on smiling. I huff and cross my arms over my chest. "Why didn't you just give it back right away?"

He says, "Two can play the game, sweetheart."

I want to knee him in the balls. Just right here, right now. Watch him double over and grab my arms to catch himself. Fingers curling into my biceps. Forehead resting in the crook of my neck.

Suddenly I can't breathe.

"You okay?" he says. Curse my fair Irish skin; I can't think a thing without it showing up all over my entire body.

"I'm fine," I snap.

"Well. Sweet dreams, then."

I shut the door in his face.

"What was that about a knight in shining armor?" says Riya.

"You shut up immediately."

Riya starts cackling, like *falls over* cackling, and Addie catches her. I'm not even paying attention; I'm too busy checking my phone. Frantically. He didn't change the language, the alarms look fine. Nothing in my address book is changed. Nothing weird texted or anything. I keep scrolling. And scrolling.

Five minutes later I get a text from "My Biggest Threat." He's programmed himself into my phone. I missed it.

> **My Biggest Threat:** what are you still doing up, young lady?

I scowl, willing my mouth not to curl up.

> **Carter:** Someone woke me up.
>
> **My Biggest Threat:** oh please. You weren't sleeping.
>
> **Carter:** Maybe I don't need a good night's sleep to beat you.

I text again, before he has the chance to respond.

> **Carter:** My biggest threat, huh?
> **My Biggest Threat:** I try to be honest.
> **Carter:** Honesty and ego are not the same
> thing.

I can picture him there in his room, arm under his head, smirking up at his phone screen, and something twists in my belly.

> **My Biggest Threat:** Not always.
> **Carter:** You are honestly insufferable.
> **My Biggest Threat:** yeah you've said that.
> **My Biggest Threat:** get your beauty sleep,
> princess.
> **Carter:** You've called me that one before
> **My Biggest Threat:** oh are you keeping track

I practically throw my phone into the nightstand drawer and slam it shut. And ignore the catcalls and suspicious looks from Riya and Addie that are stabbing daggers into me from all sides.

I don't know when exactly I fall asleep, or when exactly I wake up, but there is no break between those things from my brain, and its thinking about Reid.

Today is a group challenge. There are only fourteen of us left, and barring a major disaster on one team, there *should*

be just one of us from each team sent home after the individual challenges this week. *Barring any major disaster* being the key phrase. I slide a glance over at Reid and he is not even looking in my direction.

Andrew snaps in front of my face. "Carter."

I blink. "What?"

"Where the hell are you?"

"I'm right here."

He narrows his eyes and says, "You gonna get started on that sauce any time soon?"

I whirl around to look up at him and I'm mad that he is so much taller than I am. "Well, Andrew," I say—slow and over-enunciating, "I will be starting on the sauce when it's time to actually make the sauce."

"What?"

"You're still cooking the lamb."

"Okay?"

"So how about you focus on doing what you're gonna do, and you let me focus on what I'm gonna do."

His nostrils flare and he stands a little taller. He is the Gaston of this kitchen; he doesn't want to be told no, and that makes me want to just spend the rest of this challenge telling him no as many times as possible. "Carter, this is a group challenge and after you screwed up—"

"Let it GO. Good LORD," I say. My voice is too loud by a margin; I know, I can hear it. But there's like nothing I can do to tamp it down. "You screwed up scallops, I screwed up a meringue, we're still here and there's nothing either of us can do to turn back time." He blinks. "So how about you get your *ass* back to your lamb before you screw that up, too."

He is red, hands curled into fists, and I am high as a kite off of it.

But he goes. Because we are running out of time. Riya is smiling to herself across the kitchen while she works on roasting some green beans and garlic and Addie audibly snorts.

Reid is glancing over at me now, and his lips are twitching into an almost-smile. After thirty seconds of looking around my station, Reid crosses the kitchen. "You looking for the flour?" He holds out the bag to me, and even though it does in fact say ALL-PURPOSE FLOUR, I flip him off.

"Your loss," he says. He turns away from me and winks. He definitely did something to it. It takes me an extra two minutes to find the flour in the back, but I find it eventually, and then remember that I left the butter out to melt and took my eye off it to get back to the pantry.

I glance down at it—the perfect level of meltiness. Then glance up at Reid. Shit. Shit.

He catches my eye from where he's whisking something, biceps flexing under this tight white T-shirt, and he raises a single eyebrow.

I stare back at the butter, hands frozen. What if he did something? He can't have; this is butter. It's just butter. I sniff it, fingers digging into the bag of flour. It smells like butter. I don't think . . . oh my god, I'm being a complete basketcase.

I shut my eyes and drop a dollop into my sizzling pan, which now I'm worried has been sabotaged in some way, but the butter seems to be reacting normally to the heat, and it's not like he put iocane powder in it. Whatever he's done can't actually murder a judge.

I don't think.

I stir some salt and flour into the butter to make a roux and keep my eyes on the other spices I need for this sauce while I stir. I'm looking hard enough at them that my roux burns slightly but it's fine. It's fine, it's fine.

Reid isn't even breaking a sweat. He's cool and collected, so confident that whatever he has done to screw me today must have already happened. My sauce is probably already ruined or maybe the lamb or . . . I don't know, I don't know.

Sweat is running down my forehead, my chest; it's popping up on my wrists, of all things, and I didn't even know that was possible.

I dip my finger in the sauce before I pour it over the lamb and it tastes fine? I think? Despite the slight burning. I add a little salt, a pinch of saffron, and then it's legitimately good. But maybe whatever sabotage he's done won't come out until judging and I'll be standing there all confident, smug next to Andrew, and then the first judge will taste it and say, "This tastes like burnt rubber. Get out of my kitchen," and I will have to slit Reid's throat as I leave and then go to prison but it will be worth it.

I'm shaking hard enough as I drizzle the sauce that I get specks all over the plate.

Riya hisses, "Get it together, Carter."

"I am. I am."

Judging commences. There are no disasters.

I'm still sweating when we leave the kitchen, and there is not a hair out of place on Reid's beautifully undercut head, and I probably still look panicked when we cross the quad back to the dorm. Reid, however, is laughing.

It goes this way three days later, too, when we have the individual challenges.

Reid texts me the night before.

**My Biggest Threat:** how are you feeling about tomorrow?

**Carter:** Confident

**My Biggest Threat:** oh really

I don't respond but I can't get it out of my head. And I am just panicking all the way through my crab cakes and avocado relish, shaking so hard the whole freaking time that I drop my avocado relish twice and have to remake it. Twice. I barely plate in time. Riya keeps giving me weird looks and I wonder if she thinks I am intimidated by Andrew. Or, not worse, but still not ideal, so love struck with Reid that I can't focus.

It is neither of those things.

I am screwing up everything because I am waiting, and I hate, hate, hate waiting.

There are still too many of us for the judges to give us our individual dish evaluations aloud, which means I will be waiting some more. Shaking some more. Sweating some more. Until judging. I'll have no idea what Reid did until I know if I'm being sent home.

I barely sleep that night and can barely concentrate all through the next day, until judging. When two people go home, and those two people are not me, and now, six weeks in, we are in the final twelve.

I blow out a deep breath. Whatever he did, I am still here. This week, at least, I've won.

# CHAPTER THIRTEEN

It is two a.m. and I can't sleep. Tomorrow is another group challenge, I think, though the judges never really confirm to the degree I want them to. And I don't know if I'm super nervous about it or if I'm just tired. It's been a long several weeks. I think everyone is tired.

It seems ridiculous, though, that I am too tired to sleep. But here we are.

I am hit once again with the pang of missing home.

Em and I have texted a few times—like I could go a month and a half without really talking to her—but I barely have time with all the cramming and cooking and panic to actually jump into phone calls with her, and she's working her ass off at the pool this summer. It's hard.

It . . . it's no one's fault. But I feel lonely.

Disconnected.

Just. Tired.

I blink up at the ceiling, and I am thinking about last week, and wondering what Reid did to screw me over, because he certainly looked as though he was doing something to screw me over, was certainly just as cocky and ass-holey as ever, like he had accomplished something. Even when my dishes weren't affected and I made it through the week. Like he had won.

It's infuriating, and it vibrates under my skin.

Maybe that is why I can't sleep.

Riya is snoring like a foghorn, lying there perfectly still on her back, and here I am. I'll go into tomorrow's challenge sleep-deprived and maybe that will be the end for me. That speeds up my heart rate even further and now I'm in a semi-panic. But it's two a.m. and I am not lying here in the dark thinking about ingredients and the particular bad habits of the stove and what pan I should use next time if I wind up on sauces again, and how sautéing behaves a little differently in all this heat and humidity. I am thinking about Reid and what he can do to destroy me. How I can destroy him. I've been doing that since I got here.

Maybe that was his angle all along. The pranks were inconsequential; change her *mindset*, that will get her.

That sounds like an awful big set of machinations, though. Especially if it was his aim from the beginning. He didn't even know me when this started. I was just the grape-haired girl, indistinguishable from anyone else. There's no way, even as devious and assholey as he is, that he just picked me as his biggest competition for no reason and set out to ruin me.

DAMMIT, here we are again.

I shut my mouth tight and blow an exasperated breath out through my nose rather than screaming. No sense taking Riya down with me into this obsession-somnia.

I fling my feet over the edge of the bed and scratch my head. Maybe a thirty-minute change of scenery is in order.

At home, when I can't sleep, I slip into the kitchen and bake. I don't even like baking, really, but there is nothing better for two a.m. than hot cocoa and a blueberry muffin. That's not an option here, unfortunately. The kitchen stays locked after we leave. But what is an option is sneaking down to the common room to read.

I walk down the stairs in plaid night shorts, a bed-wrinkled black tank (both hand-me-downs from my sister), and bare feet, so quiet, apart from one rogue stair squeak, that I think no one will hear me. Unless they have supersonic hearing. But I doubt anyone is awake.

The fire is going—seriously, it must just literally always be going—and it is completely silent apart from the crackle and my breathing.

I eye the little bookshelf, hoping desperately that it has more on it than just the classics that school requires you to read. And stop short.

There's this black tuft of hair, and I can see his nose in profile. Elbow on the arm of a couch, long fingers turning pages. I can't make out the distinct features of his face, because it's dark in here except for the fire. But I don't need to. It's Reid.

I look up at the sky, silently asking whatever deity may be responsible for this, "Are you serious?"

Then I grind my teeth together and take a step back.

"Don't leave on my account," he says without looking up.

I consider leaving anyway. I don't think I want to be down here with him, especially since it's basically him keeping me awake. But . . . I kind of don't want to leave either.

So I just freeze there. My shadow is awkward, completely tall and immobile on the rug.

After about four seconds, Reid says, "Carter, come on. I'm not going to bite. Common room isn't mine."

Now I can't leave. It will look like an intentional retreat, which I guess it always would have been. But . . . I don't want it to *look* that way. I don't want him to know he's won. So I pull a random book off the shelf and head into the room.

He looks so relaxed here, in the dark with a book. Like . . . a human. Just a boy who can't sleep.

He looks up and doesn't say anything, just moves his feet from the cushion where they were planted. Giving me room to sit.

There are three other possible places to sit in this room, all comfortable, none of them near him. But that end of the couch is closest to the fire. And he moved so I could sit there. Like maybe . . . like maybe he wants me to?

Anyway. I do.

"What did you pick?" he says.

I'm actually not sure what I picked. I look down at it, as curious as he is. Oh. Somehow I landed on a book I actually do love. "Star Wars? It's about Ahsoka."

His face lights up in a way I have literally never seen it do. "Oh man, that's so kickass. Have you read it before?"

I smile against my will. "Yeah. Twice."

"I saw *The Force Awakens* in theaters a solid four times."

My mouth turns up. "Five here." I spent *so* much tip money on it. And it was worth living in a few more of Jillian's old jeans.

He gives me a little bow, conceding the victory, and I find myself turning toward him on the couch, legs criss-crossed on the cushion. His legs are too long to do that. But he rests his knee on it, the other leg planted on the floor, throws his arm over the cushion to face me. There are several inches of space between our laps, on that middle cushion.

I am aware enough of them that I almost want to back up, but I don't want to acknowledge it, any of it, at all. So I talk.

"What's in your hands?"

*"Howl's Moving Castle."*

*Oh no*, I think.

"Why?" he says, and apparently after two a.m. my filter just disintegrates into the ether because I guess I expressed my dismay out loud.

"Uh," I say. I'm creasing a page in my book now, and he is looking at my fingers like he wants to snatch them away. Like honestly, how dare I do that to a book? I think he might actually be half a second from physically grabbing my hand and tearing it away from the novel to rescue it, so I say, and his attention blinks back to my mouth, "Oh no. It's too perfect." Because it's what I am thinking. And it's too late-slash-early for rational thought.

Coming down here was a terrible idea.

He smiles, then, and sets the book to the side. "I mean, yeah. Have you seen the movie though?"

"Of course. What do you take me for?"

His teeth are at his lip and he scoots forward almost infinitesimally. The only reason I can even tell is just . . . I'm just hyper aware of it.

"Miyazaki is a legend," I say.

"That's an understatement."

I blink down at his knee and it's—it's close to mine. Really close. I don't move back, though, and I don't think he's the only one who's been closing that distance. It's like a magnet. Repellant and drawing all in one pair.

"How often do you come down here?"

He swallows and shifts, arm scratching over the fabric. "A lot. I'm not a great sleeper."

"No?"

"Nah. Stressed."

My eyebrows jump up. "You? Stressed?"

"I'm not a robot, Lane."

"Yeah but I guess . . . well. I guess that's true. Allegedly."

I really look at him then, in this thin V-neck I can basically see through, these drawstring pajama pants no one was supposed to see. His eyes are lined with red, his hair smudged, rumpled, like maybe he *was* sleeping and woke up. I wonder if he spent a night like this when I screwed with his alarm.

"Two to four, like clockwork," he says.

"So you just got down here then."

"Yeah."

"Am I interrupting?"

"Yes," he says, but he flashes me a smile.

This room, in the dark and the fire and all of it, it just feels . . . close. Too close. And I'm interrupting, which is not a thing I want to do. So I move to stand and say, "Sorry. I didn't mean—"

"No, stay," he says, and suddenly his fingers are gentle on my wrist. But pressing them to the cushion. I could move if I wanted.

I stare down at his fingers and he stares down at them. They're calloused on my skin. Rough against all these smooth little burn scars on mine.

"Sorry," he says, and it's charged.

Everything is charged, like if I move the wrong way something will shatter.

He pulls his fingers back and says, "It's just anxiety. That keeps me up."

He's giving me this so I will stay. Giving me a sentence about himself that invites a question. And he plays it right, because I relax back into the couch.

"That is . . . so at odds with literally everything about you."

"Is it?" He cocks his head.

"I don't know."

"Two to four a.m. is the perfect time to replay everything I have said in the past week that could piss literally anyone I know off, and to go over recipes that I have no hope of changing, and over all the shit that could go wrong at judging, or tomorrow during the challenge, and then when I've sorted through all that, to cycle through who I've probably pissed off this week again."

I laugh. "So you think about me a lot between two and four then."

The expression on his face shifts, then. It's a small change. But it's there. He straightens a little, eyes become more focused. He's looking at me with the same concentration he uses in the kitchen. And I can feel it under my skin. I flush.

"If it helps, I was up thinking about you," I say, like that will make it better. And I resolve, in that second, never to come out of my room again before six in the morning.

"Yeah?" he says. His mouth tugs up, a dimple I didn't know he had popping.

"I was thinking about what on earth you did to me this last week, and how you failed so spectacularly at it because I'm still here."

His eyebrow twitches. Then he just starts laughing.

"Reid, good lord, people are sleeping."

He shuts his mouth and throws his head back over the arm of the couch, and his leg stretches out the tiniest bit, calf brushing mine. He's still shaking, laughing. Just silent this time. I push his leg, and he sits up.

His eyes are almost literally sparkling.

"What did you do?" I say.

"Nothing."

He wipes a tear from the corner of his eye and gasps in a breath.

"Yeah, that sounds truthful."

"I'm serious, Carter."

"Okay."

"I didn't do anything to you."

He's calmed down now, leaning over, elbows on his knees, grinning like an idiot.

"So just out of the goodness of your heart, you—" I stop short. He looks about twice as wicked as he ever did, and I can feel it radiating off him. "You really didn't do anything to me."

He taps his nose.

"But . . ." I say, narrowing my eyes. "Not out of the goodness of your heart."

"Sweet pea, I never do anything out of the goodness of my heart."

"You were looking at me all weird, though, and like moving my stuff and . . . that is psychological warfare."

He smiles so wide it only makes me angrier, and then he spreads his arms out. Like, *Duh, Carter. Know thine enemy.*

I stand, face screwed into something I cannot even imagine the look of, except I am sure it looks pissed.

"How can you be that mad at me? I didn't even do anything!"

"Don't even start that with me, you asshole."

I go to stomp off, and he says, "Don't forget your book."

I flip him off and leave.

Nothing helps me get to sleep.

# CHAPTER FOURTEEN

I am still mad when I wake up.

I have been mad all night, if the strain in my neck is any indication. It feels like I slept on it wrong, but it was just me and this pillow from the time I furiously dove back into this bed, and this is a completely averagely fluffed pillow. So it's not that. It's gotta be hypertension.

I don't think I've ever been this mad this often in my entire life. And now my body is paying for it.

It is Reid's fault that I wake up sore. Just add that to the list.

Riya stays on the other side of the room while she gets dressed for breakfast and keeps sneaking glances at me.

"You okay there?" she says.

I grumble, "I'm fine."

Riya raises an eyebrow. "You sure about that?"

"It's just—" I snort out of frustration and Riya says, "Yes, you sound very okay."

"It's Reid."

This *Ha! I knew it!* brand of smirk lights up her face and I groan.

"It's not like that. It's just he's . . . he's been a total asshole to me."

The smirk immediately darkens and she says, "Do I need to kill a boy?"

"Probably not. But I reserve the right to change that answer."

"What's the latest?" she says.

I open my mouth to give a scathing level of dirt but then nothing comes out because what am I supposed to say? *Well, Riya, he did NOTHING TO ME over the past couple of days. A vicious, targeted nothing. Can you believe that? Kill him immediately.*

Riya just waits there, eyebrows raised, expectantly, and I *also* can't tell her the actual things he did to me because that would entail confessing that we have both been sabotaging each other, which, when it comes down to it, means that we have both been *epic fanfare noise* cheating.

"It's nothing," I say.

Riya rolls her eyes. "And here we are again. You guys should probably just make out and get it over with."

I laugh. "Okay. When you and—"

"Don't say it. Do not. Say it."

I grin.

"We have a challenge in like twenty minutes. We should probably. You know. Focus on that."

I say, "Ah, the tables have turned."

"Well, I needed to know if I had to commit murder before we went down to the kitchens; that was critical information."

"Hm," I say. "Well. Fair."

And now the impending challenge has my stomach all in knots. "Are you nervous?" I say.

"For today?"

"Yeah."

Riya shrugs and runs her hand through her hair. "I mean, I guess. I'm always a little nervous."

"You *never* seem nervous."

A smile splits her face. "No?"

"Even freaking Andrew is afraid of you."

She says, "Oh, please, he's not afraid of me," but she tosses her hair while she says it. She should be proud. That douche seems incapable of being intimidated.

"You know he is."

She looks down at her nails and says, "Well. He should be." Then goes in search of a decent pair of pants to wear downstairs.

"I'm nervous," I say.

"I know." I raise an eyebrow in response. "You don't hide it super well." Riya laughs and I just shrug.

"That was never one of my strong suits, no."

"What are you so freaked out about?"

"Oh, just . . ." I can feel the dread grabbing at my bones. That familiar thing that says *Carter, you want something too much. You want something that everyone else here wants too and what makes you that special?* Like I'm arrogant to even go for it. "There's eleven other people here. And it feels so small now but it feels like so many people, too."

"Yeah."

"I just . . . damn, I need a break from this place for five seconds."

"Tell me about it," she says. "All cooking all the time, your friends are your competition." She pulls a shirt over her head. Then says, "It's . . . a lot."

"Yeah," I say. And I get dressed and go downstairs.

There's hardly any breakfast left; most people are putting their stuff up and heading over to the kitchen by the time we get to the cafeteria, so there's basically just time to grab a couple granola bars and go.

I snag one for me and one for her, and Reid looks over at us before he leaves. "What happened, Lane?" His long legs carry him close to me much faster than I would have anticipated. "You oversleep?"

I purse my lips. "No. Some of us know how to set alarms on our phones."

He barks out a laugh. "Do you, though? Eleven minutes until challenge."

I keep my eyes locked on his while I take a slow bite of my granola bar. Luxuriate in the brown sugar and the oats and chocolate chips. His Adam's apple bobs when he swallows. "Then you'd better go, Reid. Don't want to be late."

Reid grinds his teeth together for an instant, eyes on my granola bar. Or something near it. "Walk with me," he says.

Heat crawls up my face and I bet I'm blushing and there is just no reason for that. Riya is beside me and I can feel her nearly vibrating.

"I'm sorry, I don't think I'm up for psychological torture today."

"I swear I won't torture you," he says. "There's hardly any time for that on a walk this short." His mouth tips up.

He's so adorably adorable right now that I almost give into it, and since when did I start thinking of Reid as adorable? EXTREMELY since when did that matter in any way? Now I'm mad. Mad about the adorableness, I guess, and mad that that thought has even crossed my mind, and mad because I barely got any sleep and I've just been mad for a while, and so I say, "Reid." My voice comes out hard. "I'm walking with Riya. I'm not interested."

He blinks. And something in his face falls. "Oh. Yeah, okay. I'll uh, see you at the kitchen then."

I take a very hard bite of my granola bar, hard enough that I bite my tongue, but I have to just suffer it in silence. So I stand there, eyes watering so no one will know that I have legitimately just injured myself on my hatred for that boy. And when he seems like he's a safe distance ahead of us, Riya and I go.

She doesn't ask about it, even though I can see her biting her tongue to keep from it, and I appreciate that.

Because, frankly, I'm a little confused myself.

The one thing that's so very enthusiastically burrowing under my skin is the frustration of all of it, and namely this: walking across the quad, minutes ticking down until challenge time, I realize I didn't put five seconds of thought last night into today's challenge. I haven't been googling technique or streaming cooking shows half as often as I should.

I'm so mad at myself right now, because somewhere along the line, I started devoting more brainpower to him than to what I actually *want*. My fingers curl into fists, because this was me. He didn't crawl into my brain and reprogram it; I did that all on my own.

Well, no more. If Reid Yamada wants my attention, he can earn it, because from here on out, my brain is nothing but flour and sugar and butter and flank steaks and ten billion different kinds of bizarre reductions. I grit my teeth before we open the door.

Riya stands beside me in the kitchen, which looks so empty now. It's funny, because I would have definitely thought before that twelve chefs in a kitchen was ridiculously overcrowded, but now my skin practically tingles at the promise of all this open space in which to move.

We are the last ones here. The judges still wait until the clocks hits nine a.m. to start, and the moment Dr. Kapoor starts talking, I shut my eyes to find my zen. I need it today.

Today, whatever happens, I will do nothing but focus.

"Well," he says. "Only a dozen of you left. I wish to commend you all on making it this far. But there is still a long road ahead to get to that scholarship."

My heart sinks at that, hanging out in the bottom of my stomach like lead. The thought in my head that whispers: *This is a waste, a waste, a waste. You're never going to get it.* I mentally bat it away and blink ahead at the judges.

"I assume we're all comfortable with the way things have worked up until this point. Mystery ingredients and time cut short and judging both individually and in our groups."

This feels like a sentence that precedes the word *but*.

"But today," says Dr. Kapoor, and if I wasn't so freaking nervous, I would be proud of myself for predicting the next word. Like a psychic. "Today, everything changes."

A little rustle goes through the group and I glance at Riya, then across the kitchen at Reid, who is very definitely not looking at me.

I look back up front. No distractions today.

Even if he does look sad, like a tall, aggressive puppy.

No. Distractions.

"Starting today," Dr. Freeman cuts in, "the individual challenges will be eliminated. To be resurrected at a later date, but from here on out, while there will indeed be two weekly challenges, you will not be performing any of them on your own."

Andrew's smug face pops into my head and suddenly I'm not just nervous—I'm actually worried. If it's all group stuff from now until who-knows-when, he could completely screw us. Lord save me from overconfident white boys.

Maybe Riya's spine of steel will rescue us. If anything possibly can.

The energy in the room is immediately different—the tension is actually tangible on the air. I'm tapping my fingers on my thigh and have to consciously tell myself to unclench my jaw. It's sore already.

"The group challenges will also be eliminated."

Now, I frown. Because what does that even leav—

"You will be divided into teams of two," she says. "Teams are already assigned and were drawn randomly; do not try to appeal the decision. I can assure you, you will be turned down. Both challenges per week will be completed with your teammate, and the first challenge begins in about four minutes. Are we clear?"

Blood is rushing through my head, heart working hard to pump it all through my veins. There's nothing to be nervous about, there's nothing to be nervous about. I could get paired with Riya.

"First team is Riya Khatri and Will Malik." Riya actually squeals a little bit and Will's smile is bright enough to light the kitchen on fire.

My heart sinks a little further. Okay, well maybe Addie or Tess— "Addie Thomas and Andrew Olan."

Addie's lips thin, but she throws her shoulders back and heads over to him. Godspeed. It goes like that until everyone I know is paired off—Tess and some girl from the other team I haven't gotten to know very well. The girl Addie was flirting with and the tiny boy with the glasses. A couple other kids I've hung out with at meal time. And then that's it.

I make eye contact with him before Dr. Freeman says it, and I bet I look as exhausted and pissed as he does.

"Reid Yamada and Carter Lane."

Of course.

Of freaking *course*.

I cross the kitchen to him, stand in his personal space. And accept my fate.

# CHAPTER FIFTEEN

He doesn't turn his head to look at me. He just glances down out of the corner of his eye.

"Well," he says.

"Well," I say.

And that is *all* we say before the judge presents the challenge: it's back to one of the original formats. Secret ingredient stuff. The box isn't terrible, all things considered: onion, Panko, purple carrots, and Warheads. Like, those weird burn-your-taste-buds-off candies that no one eats unless they've been dared to see how long they can hold one in their mouth without puckering.

I always won those contests as a kid. *Always.*

I can do this.

They give us thirty minutes.

Thirty minutes will hardly be enough time to chisel through this rock wall between Reid and me so we can actually speak through it, but whatever; we will make do.

"So," I say.

He turns to face me and says, "What are we gonna do with this?"

I stare down at the box, partly to process what's in it and partly just to avoid having to look at Reid. I grab the carrots and turn, because maybe we can just . . . get through this without having to talk to each other at all. I can slice some carrots and he can crust some meat in that Panko and we'll just move around each other seamlessly and come up with a coherent dish.

I go to take a step and Reid's hand is around my wrist. Not hard. It's a question he's asking with his fingers.

"Hey," he says. His voice, on the other hand, is pretty sharp.

"What?" I say.

"You wanna tell me where you're going with those?"

"The sink, Reid," I say. "Unless you have something against washing produce."

He narrows his eyes. "We should talk about what we're gonna cook."

"I don't see why we have to talk at all."

"Carter."

"What?"

His nostrils flare and he drops my wrist. "I thought we'd kind of made some headway here."

I shrug. "Yeah, well. That was before you admitted to conducting psychological sabotage on me."

"You have *got* to be kidding me."

"What?" I say. "Is it that unreasonable that I'm pissed at you?"

"No,' he says. "It's that unreasonable that we've wasted two entire minutes arguing when we should have been figuring out what our dish is gonna be, so are you gonna play or did you want to just fight for a while?"

I swallow. Blink up at him.

"I'll wait," he says. "I'm sure both of us will have plenty of time to come up with witty retorts we could have fired in this discussion while we're flying home at the end of the week."

I blow out a frustrated breath. "Fine," I say. "Fine."

"So what," he says, "are you doing with those carrots?"

"Why don't you tell me?" I say. "You're so concerned with working together. I bet you have just a million ideas that are better than mine."

"Not a chance, cream puff. What's your grand plan?"

"I just . . ." Suddenly, I'm totally self-conscious. He's looking at me like he expects something of me. Like he is completely confident I'm going to meet those expectations, and how is that so nerve-wracking?

Except I don't know. Suddenly, when it's not just me in my head, running through possibilities with my own brain and my own food and my own stove, it's terrifying. What if I'm wrong and it's stupid and . . .

Reid's eyebrow slowly arches.

I clear my throat and stand a little taller. Summon some bravado I do not feel. "I thought," I say. Then I glance down at the kitchen floor. Blow out a breath. Make myself meet that stare of appraisal that's *almost* trying to be reassuring. "I thought we could roast these carrots in a balsamic kind of thing. Maybe crush up some of the Warheads in that."

"Yeah, I like that," he says, and it takes everything in me not to say, *YOU DO? HOORAY* like his approval matters so damn much.

It doesn't.

He doesn't.

I just smile, a *little*. Allow myself a single tip of the mouth.

"Why don't you do the carrots, then?" he says. "I can do something with the Panko on beef. Fry them up and we can do a reduction over it, too."

I bristle, even though there's no reason for me to. There's literally nothing in his statement I can get offended by; it's just that he's already moving like it's decided, and I am annoyed that he's so confident. I'm annoyed that I feel like he's basically in charge here and I'm the assistant. Even though I don't think he would see it that way. I don't think anyone but me would view it like that.

But *god*, that's how this feels. That's how it's felt every time I've stepped into this kitchen, clawing for something that probably won't even be mine.

Like I'm just . . . listening.

It's bullshit, I think. He asked me what I was *going* to do, not what I *maybe wanted* to do. He pushed me to tell him, to just decide right then and there, and then planned his own thing around mine. But when I get in my head, I can't see through my own panic. I just—lord, I am being ridiculous.

This whole room, judges at the front, and judgey people milling around and around, just makes me shrink.

I'm annoyed at Reid. For no real reason except that he knows what he wants and he knows who he is and he knows what he's going to do (not just what he wants to do, what he's *going* to do) in any given situation, and it works. I'm annoyed, more than anything, that this is now suddenly going smoothly.

Maybe I want to hate him.

Maybe there's just a weird comfort in wanting to strangle him, I don't know.

But I know that all this is really getting under my skin. I pull out a sharp knife and go at these carrots and I am irritated.

I'm irritated!

At what!

I huff and Reid slides a glance at me.

"You sure those are thin enough, there, sugar?" he says, and now I know exactly why I am irritated.

"Do *you* want to come over here and do it, Yamada?"

"Ooh, *Yamada*. Struck a nerve?"

"Shut up and slice your beef or whatever you're doing."

I glance over at him and he rolls his eyes. "I'm not saying you don't know how to cut carrots, I was just trying to get a rise—"

"Maybe it shouldn't be beef."

I'm aware we're having this argument over everyone, and several of the judges are actually raising their eyebrows, but time is running low and god, I *cannot stand this*.

"I'm already slicing beef," he says.

"You've sliced two pieces."

"Right, which is—"

"I'm just saying we didn't even consider anything else."

He clenches his teeth and drops the knife onto the butcher's block. Grabs either side and says, "Would you like to go through an itemized list of every meat that exists, Carter? Right here, right now?"

I groan and slice my carrots.

"Chicken, beef, pork, fish—oh wait, do you want me to be specific?"

"I'm just saying maybe we should have taken half a second—"

"Lest you hadn't noticed," he says, and I can hear the irritation in his voice. It's verging on anger, which probably matches mine, "that timer is ticking down, and everyone in here is already *cooking*."

"Well, lest *you* hadn't noticed, we haven't even talked about the vinaigrette and what's going in it and neither of us has any idea as to whether it'll go with both the carrots and the beef, especially considering the candy."

"Oh my god," he says.

"What?"

"I'm slicing this beef!"

"FINE," I say. "The beef is fine but we need to communicate on this reduction or vinaigrette or whatever it is before we wreck everything."

"*Obviously.*"

I almost nick my fingertip, I'm moving so fast cutting these carrots, and I'm not paying the attention I should because I'm paying too much attention to being mad at Reid. Again. When I absolutely swore I was done with all of that. I'm a little embarrassed about it, to be honest. Because Will and Riya are doing fine. Even freaking Andrew and Addie seem to be cooperating, and we have twenty-one minutes left, and it's looking most likely that I will be serving up a nice fried plate of Reid's actual throat to the judges; this is not professional.

I wonder if they'll dock points for us acting like jerks to each other.

If they even can.

I don't know.

I don't know.

What I do know is that these carrots are, indeed, *thin enough*, and that he isn't any better at this than me.

At least, I tell that to myself over and over and over.

When I'm finished with the carrots, I head over to the butcher's block that Reid is occupying and just leave them in a bowl.

His beef is done and he's mixing up some Panko and egg and spices to coat it.

"Do you want me to start on the reduction?" I say.

He's stirring so fast that I can see the muscles in his forearms flexing, veins popping. I struggle with the whole swallowing thing. Reid is unbearable half the time, but he's hot *all* the time.

I probably look like a frazzled, sweaty, cotton candy head.

He says, "Hmm?" just whipping that Panko mix around again and again and again. His jaw is clenched and he's stirring a lot more enthusiastically than he needs to, I think, so he's probably still mad.

Whatever.

All we need to do is get through this; we don't need to make it to the other side as best friends.

You don't need to like each other to cook together.

"Should I get started," I say, "on the reduction?"

Reid glances up from the bowl. Swallows. He cuts a look at the carrots and says, "Yeah, just—just go for it."

"You want to talk about it?"

"We're short on time; whatever. I trust you. I'm sure it'll be fine."

Okay, so We Need To Do This As A Team Reid is no longer interested in cooperation either. Fine by me.

I head to the stoves, right beside Will, to work on melting these stupid Warheads, and Reid hits up a different one a few feet from me to fry up his beef medallions.

My pulse slows just having a divide between us.

Will is working on something that I think looks like chicken. Maybe pork. It's ridiculous that I can't tell but the cut is weird, whatever it is, and a lot of stuff looks kind of similar when it's raw. He says, "You, uh, doing okay over there?"

"I'm fine."

"You're not gonna go all Sweeney Todd on loverboy?"

"I wasn't planning on it but there's a lot of knives around here."

He snorts. "Try to refrain from murder in the kitchen. At the very least, no jugular hits. If you get blood in this masterpiece, I will be *very* put out."

I smirk. "Okay, I'll give it a shot, but no promises."

Riya brushes past Will, and he glances up from his skillet, just for a half second, just enough for me to see his eyes flick toward her.

I dig my teeth into my lip, smile, and think about that for a moment. A little mental reset.

Then I focus.

The Warheads melt down surprisingly easily after I crush them, which is nice, but damn, sour blue raspberry is it a difficult flavor to work with.

Reid says, "You done on that yet?"

"No."

"Let me help."

"How. You wanna stir?"

"No, I want to get it done; we have less than ten minutes."

I say, "Listen—"

But he's already over here, tasting some of the stuff off a spoon.

"Dude this is terrible," he says, and before I can say, "I HAVEN'T STIRRED SINCE I ADDED SALT, REID," he tosses a handful of salt in.

"SHIT," I yell.

We are rewarded with a *very* sharp look from a judge, but come on. Like I'm the only one dropping four-letter words in this kitchen.

"That needed salt and you know it," he says.

"Yeah which is why I *added some*, Reid."

"But—"

"Taste it!" I say, and I hold up the new sauce.

"Oh no," he says immediately. "Oh shit, oh shit."

"Maybe you should *listen*, Reid."

"Maybe this isn't the *time*, Lane."

I let out a muffled scream and say, "UGH NO, I forgot to put the carrots in."

"They're already in. We can let them finish with the sauce on them."

"Thank you," I say through gritted teeth.

"What the hell are we gonna do about this sauce?"

"That *you* screwed up?"

"YES, CARTER, GOD."

I scramble for some sugar to balance it, and he reaches for some habanero powder; maybe the spicy will work with the salt and the sweet and the balsamic we have going. I have *no* idea.

I think I dirty about four hundred spoons testing it in various underwhelming stages.

Time ticks down, second by second, and by the end, we are both huddled over the same skillet, desperate for it to just . . . be tolerable. All we can hope for is tolerable.

I add another sprinkle of the habanero.

"What . . . what do you think?" I say. I stick my finger in my mouth and I'm not stoked about it, but I don't think there's anything else to be done.

Reid tastes it. "Dammit. It's . . . it's fine. It'll have to be fine."

We mix it with the mostly roasted carrots and opt not to drizzle it over the Panko beef with tiny bits of onion in the crust. We just set the beef on top of the carrot mixture when it comes out, and drizzle the plate with the sauce.

Shit.

I'm so nervous when the judging begins that I am sweating everywhere, and it's not because of the heat in the kitchen.

I can barely hear them as they go, team by team, down the line. They have varying degrees of compliments and criticisms—with more strong reactions one way or the other to the Warhead stuff. Riya and Will's, of course, is magical. Because everyone can see it but them, and *they* are like this Disney prince and princess of a team. Addie's is killer, too. The other few teams are fine, but the reactions buzz in my ears—all I can pick out are positive and negative tones. At least one or two of them get decidedly negative.

When they get to us, they decide that the beef is cooked well, the carrots are lovely, and the vinaigrette/reduction/ Warhead crap/WHATEVER IT IS is . . . weird. It's just . . . weird.

*Weird* is not an adjective that makes me feel good.

*Weird* clearly has Reid on-edge because his hands are actually shaking as we leave, his teeth grinding together. He's always like the picture of arrogance, so now I'm even more nervous than I was. Which is saying something.

We don't speak when we get back to the dorm.

Fine.

Good.

I don't want to speak to him.

He is definitely not the reason I keep checking my phone until I fall asleep.

# CHAPTER SIXTEEN

I wake up to a text, but not from Reid.

And it's fine.

Of course it's fine. Literally why wouldn't it be fine?

It's my sister.

> **Jillian:** HAVE YOU WON YET, BUG
>
> **Carter:** NOPE
>
> **Jillian:** Well get on it I miss you and also no
> one can cook
>
> **Carter:** YOU get on it. I have confidence in
> your ability to turn on an oven
>
> **Jillian:** UGH
>
> **Jillian:** Well. I love you bb. Kick absolute ass.
>
> **Carter:** <3 <3 <3

I don't say: *Well Jill I'm fine I think I'm fine but there's this guy I can't stop thinking about, and I think teaming up is going to kill us both and also the longer I stay here, the more I think I got here on a fluke. I'll be home any effing minute ok?*

Because I don't want her to know that I'm panicking. That it's gotten to the point that every time I walk into that kitchen, it feels like a sentencing, not a gift.

I pick at my pilling shirt as I walk around outside in the heat and make my brain just slow. Take a second.

I want five minutes free of panicking. And wondering how a girl who's used nothing but clearance pans and on-sale cheap meat and . . . shit, basically, to cook with, who's never taken extra classes outside home-ec because, SURPRISE, even saying *unaffordable* is like ha. Hahaha. Understatement, meet my mouth.

But being here, where I am now, feels impossible. And the closer I get to the end, the more impossible it feels.

I keep seeing Reid, cocky and good and just assuming I'm on his level, pushing me forward, and I think: *You, Reid. You should be here.*

Riya, pushing Andrew around and destroying every challenge, Addie and this total joy that comes over her in the kitchen, so thoroughly that it's like she forgets the pressure of everything and sinks into it.

And then. Here I am.

And it's all just—terrifying.

I shove my hands down into my pockets and try to think of something else, anything else.

Then I hear laughter floating up from the trees. "Will, you can't *say that out loud.*"

"Why not? You're the only one here and you're not gonna judge me for it."

"Who said I wouldn't judge you for it? I'm judging you."

Will's laugh rings out as I round the corner and find them sitting on this picnic bench, facing each other, almost touching.

Riya jumps up as soon as she sees me and points. "Carter is here and she will judge you with me."

Will glances up at me and waves, leaning forward on that bench as soon as Riya stands, still leaning when she sits.

"Yeah," I say. "I judge you."

"You don't even know what I said," says Will.

"He said he—"

"I said I hate cats. I hate literally everything about cats, and if I could travel back in time and create a catless world, I would do it."

"Oh my god, I *am* judging you," I say.

"Cats hate you. Your cat wants to eat you alive and steal your soul. And if it can't do that, well it's at least gonna knock your shit off the counter just to watch you have to retrieve it."

Riya says, "What did CATS EVER DO TO YOU?"

"Cats never did anything to me because I refuse to be alone with one."

"You're *afraid* of cats then," I say.

Will narrows his eyes. "I like to take precautions around my enemies."

Riya stands again and Will's hand moves to curl around the back of her leg, fingers just barely resting there against her skin. "Where you going?" he says. It's quiet, and I actually blush hearing it.

"Off with someone who doesn't hate animals."

"It's not *all animals*," he says, and Riya rolls her eyes and steps over the bench to link arms with me.

Will's mouth curls up, eyes all mischief when he laughs, and Riya waves a fake-offended good-bye to him.

We walk off together, her arm in mine like we're back in middle school, and I say, "Well, you can't date him now. He hates cats."

Riya laughs, or puffs out air, really. "There's a hundred reasons I can't date Will. Cats are in, like, the top fifty."

"Please," I say. "That boy is so head over heels for you I'm surprised he can walk straight."

"You don't know Will," she says.

"Okay, but I know what *COMPLETELY DESTROY ME, PLEASE* looks like."

Riya shakes her head. "I've seen him give that look to like a dozen girls, Carter."

"I've only seen him give it to you."

She half smiles, like she doesn't want to, but she can't help it. She glances back over her shoulder to watch him walk away and says, "Well. That's because I'm the only person he knows here."

"You'd think that would be prime no-strings-attached-hookup time then. Is all I'm saying. And yet."

Riya furrows her brow. Like she hadn't quite thought of that. "Hm," is all she says.

We're mostly quiet, slowly looping the quad. Riya is lost in thought—over Will or the competition, I'm not sure. And I quickly get back to the business of stressing out about tomorrow, like that will help anything.

Stressing out, after that, about elimination. We did not perform at peak level the other day with our *weird reduction* and I don't know how to fix it, don't even know if it's possible. I'm afraid even trying would only make it worse. Though, how could it get any worse?

I am the personification of stress.

Riya says, "You okay?"

And I say, "I'm fine."

Just as feet pound up the pavement behind us, and Reid runs by, on Riya's side.

He glances back when I say, "Thought you didn't run in the middle of the day."

"Full of surprises, Lane."

He doesn't even slow, just keeps running, and I bite my lip watching his back.

"Uh-huh," says Riya.

I flip her off.

She laughs.

And Reid continues to run.

# CHAPTER SEVENTEEN

I don't want to think about the elimination last night.

We had another pretty much cake challenge the night before last, and Reid and I were . . . better. By *better*, I don't men *good* by any definition of the word, but not actively trying to tear each other's throats out the entire time, so that's. Well. Something.

Still. We're off, and nothing is flowing like it should and *no one* thinks we can just go on like this. Toes on the line of aggression.

We still haven't talked. Still haven't gotten shit sorted out that honestly, I recognize now, we *definitely* need to get sorted out.

And I was clearly an idiot thinking this wouldn't affect it.

Because obviously, it does, and it has.

We were in the bottom two teams last night: us and that freckled girl Addie keeps flirting with and whoever her teammate was. We skated through, but we . . . we are not going to skate through again. Not on barely tolerating each other.

Not on *weird*.

I blow out a long breath and poke at my dinner. The next challenge is tomorrow morning, and I need to talk to him before then or we're out. And everyone knows it.

I stand from the table, square my shoulders, and walk to where Reid is sitting,

"Hey," I say.

He raises an eyebrow. "Hey."

"We need to talk."

He sets down the Coke in his hand and says, "You're gonna condescend to speak to me now?"

I want to swallow all the words I'd planned back into my throat, because the anger just boils right back up. But I don't. I say, "You planning on insomnia again tonight?"

Reid looks at the table. Considers. Drums his fingers on the hard surface. Then says, "Two, like clockwork."

"What if I came down to the common room and interrupted it?"

Reid sighs and meets my eyes. "Okay. Yeah. I'll see you."

He leaves.

I set my alarm for two, even though I'm pretty sure my internal clock will wake me up. And it does—1:45 and I'm lying there, blinking into the dark.

I'm sure Riya appreciates not being wrenched from sleep at this ungodly hour, so that's . . . good, I guess.

Very little is good before, like, ten in the morning, though.

So I'm not enthusiastic.

I slide on a sweatshirt over this tank top, so it's that and pajama bottoms for this clandestine meeting. Very fancy, very seductive.

And slip downstairs.

I'm there a few minutes early, but Reid's already waiting for me.

He's reading something I can't see from here, and I have this annoying surge of something positive I can't put a name to in my chest. Something I quiet before I can pinpoint. But I like people who read. It's instinctive.

I shake my head.

"Hey, Lane," he says without looking up from his book. He's not whispering, but his voice is low enough I'm not concerned about waking anyone up.

"Reid," I say.

I walk softly over to him in my socks, padding on the fancy old rug, and he just silently slides his feet from where they were kicked up on the back of the couch to the floor. So once again, I wind up sitting beside him at two a.m. by the fire.

I take a couple deep breaths, because for whatever reason, suddenly I feel like I need to. And sit. I pull my knees to my chest and my sweatshirt down over my knees, then turn toward him.

He licks his thumb and turns the page. "You cold?" he says, glancing up at me.

"Not really."

He doesn't respond.

"What are you reading?"

Now that I'm used to the quiet in the room, every sentence, even though we're keeping our voices down, sounds like a whipcrack. It makes everything feel extremely close in here. Han and Leia in the trash compactor. Walls closing in.

And Luke, I think. Was in that scene. And the wookiee. Anyway.

He waits until he finishes the page he's on before slipping a bookmark between the pages and closing the book, then looking up. He sets it on the end table.

"*Howl's Moving Castle*, still?"

"Nah," he says. "Finished *Howl's*. You ever read anything by Jemisin?"

I shake my head.

"*The Hundred Thousand Kingdoms*. Really good."

I say, "I didn't have you pegged as a dude who was so into magic."

He kind of smiles. "No? Even with all the *Avatar* references? And *Howl's*?"

"I don't know, I just didn't."

"You have much to learn, young Padawan."

I roll my eyes, but I'm smiling, and see *this*—this is why Reid Yamada is the most confusing person on the planet. Because this was how it felt the other night, too. Like I was having a human conversation with a real live person, and we actually might have a shred of a prayer at getting along. And then it's back to hate.

Or anger.

Maybe they're not exactly the same thing.

"You thirsty?" he says.

I open my mouth to say no, but he picks up two mugs I hadn't noticed on the end table and hands one to me.

"Oh," I say. "Yeah, thanks."

It's cocoa, apparently. In summer in Georgia. But nighttime always makes cocoa seem appropriate.

"Wow, this is actually . . . this is *really* good."

He laughs and takes a drink of his. "Don't seem so surprised."

"I'm just saying. It's exceptional."

"You wanna know my secret?"

"I do."

"Nestlé."

Now I'm laughing. "Ah, box mix. You know how to spoil a girl."

"Don't say I never did anything for you. I *did* use *real milk* for this in the cafeteria microwave."

I put my hand to my chest and say, "Oh! You shouldn't have."

Then we're both just quietly smiling, this understanding passing between us that we would be laughing if the circumstance allowed.

"Why are you like this?" I say. It just pops out of my mouth, because it's two in the morning, and oh how soon my never-coming-out-of-my-room-before-six-a.m. vow was cast aside.

Reid raises one eyebrow and takes a slow drink. "You'll have to be more specific."

"Just like . . . like *this*. Like. A person."

"Well, I am a human person, Lane. This is how I'm programmed to interact. Though that's exactly what a robot would tell you, I guess. You wanna Turing test me?"

I roll my eyes. "No, I just mean . . . I mean usually we're like at each other's throats and you're a total asshole to me, and then under the guise of darkness, you turn into someone who's actually likeable."

"Likeable?" His eyebrows shoot about up into his hair-line. "I'm marking this day on my calendar."

"Shut up," I say, but I'm grinning into my cocoa. Against my will. I want to be scowling.

"Honestly, I think two have been playing *real well* at this game, princess."

I blush. At the dart of shame there, and I think, at the nickname. "There you go again with the *princess*."

His voice is quiet, a little different, when he says, "You really hate the nicknames?"

I don't answer, because I don't exactly know how to. What, exactly, is the answer to that question?

"That one, at least?" he pushes.

I hear myself saying, "No. Whatever," because *princess* I do not find annoying. Although I find the non-annoyance annoying so it's a little complicated. "I could do without *cream puff,* though."

He actually snorts and says, "Noted."

"We've both been asses to each other," I say.

"Ha, yeah, understatement."

I sigh and look up at the ceiling. "Do you hate me?"

When I look back down at Reid, he has the most remarkable frown on his face. This deeply concerned absolute masterwork of a furrow that has me leaning toward him, wanting to smooth it out.

"No," he says. My spine pops up straight again. "You piss me the *hell* off sometimes, like more often than not, but . . ." Now he's kind of laughing. I have to assume because that, as well, is a major understatement. "Lane, I do not hate you." He pauses, staring down at the mug in his hands. "Do you?" he says. "Hate me?"

I take longer to answer than he does. Wonder if the frown lines on my forehead are as pronounced as the ones that were on his. Wonder if he's leaning forward, too. If he wants to brush them away with his thumb.

"I . . . I did," I settle on.

I meet his eyes, and there's something that I would swear, under different circumstances with a different person, was a flash of disappointment.

"I don't think I do now."

His eyes are back to neutral, and his face is open. Maybe in the same way everyone's face is a little more open than they want in the middle of the night. Maybe more than that.

"Well then," he says. "You and I are going to need to start working together. Like. Actually working together, none of this tiptoeing around each other shit."

"Yeah," I say.

"So let's start over."

I smile.

He holds out his hand. "Reid Yamada."

I take it and we shake. One firm movement of our hands.

"Carter Lane."

He does that lopsided smirk thing that makes me a little mad and kind of lights me up in a different way all at once, and for like half a second, his thumb brushes over the crook of mine when he slides his hand back. And it doesn't . . . it doesn't feel like starting over completely.

I clear my throat and cross my ankles under my sweatshirt.

"I'll give you three questions," he says.

"Like a game?"

"Like a game. Three for three. Friends know things about each other."

"Okay," I say, and I drain the last of my mug, then disentangle myself from my own sweatshirt. I criss-cross my legs on the cushion and just look at him. "What's your biggest fear?"

"Ooh," he says. "Hitting hard, I like it. You want like the big existential fears or the tangible ones?"

"Either. Both."

He smiles. "Okay, but I expect to get as good as I give here."

"Deal."

"Existential fears. Like actual deepest, darkest, this-would-be-my-hell fear. I don't know, I'm uh, I'm pretty shit at losing people. Just terrified of it all the time, I guess."

He scratches at the back of his head, and I want to say, "Who did you lose?" but I know that's weird and invasive, and before I even could, even if I wanted to, he says, "And the less uncomfortable, but just as truthful answer, is rats."

I do let out a laugh at that. "Rats? Like just the little squeaking things?"

"Rats are vicious, man. And their beady little eyes and twitching and—" He literally shudders.

"Of all the things you could be mortally afraid of. Honestly, rats?"

"Oh god, you should have seen me when a rat ran through our kitchen when some ridiculous weather was driving them indoors. I legit screamed. Like jumped up onto a chair and everything."

I am doing that silent, shaking laugh thing. "How old were you?"

He busts out a laugh that is way too loud for this time of night and says, "Sixteen, it was last year."

And now I'm just dying. The silent, shaking laugh thing has turned into the silent, shaking cry-laugh thing and it's a hot minute before either of us can compose ourselves enough for him to ask his question.

"If you didn't want to be a chef, what would you be? Don't pick something dumb and practical unless you really do dream of being something dumb and practical."

I blink. I guess I've never really thought of that before. It's been "go to cooking school, be a chef," for so long, so deep in my bones, that I honestly haven't considered an alternative. But then the thought blinks into my mind: "BMX."

"What?" he says.

"BMX like biking. It's not part of my actual soul like food is, but I'm *really good* at bikes. I grew up in this neighborhood that was like almost all boys, and none of us had any money, so we spent most of our time on these trash bicycles out by the dirt hills. Which was actually technically a construction site that none of us had any business hanging out around but *man,* could you get some air off some of those."

"You are full of surprises," he says. "I'm really impressed."

I'm blushing again, and I don't want him to notice so I throw out a question that I'm immediately annoyed I wasted one on, just for the quickness of it. "What's your favorite color?"

"Oh, boo, hiss," he says, but it's very good-natured. Like, his face is actually relaxed for once; even his posture is relaxed. Spread out over his side of the chair—one arm slung over the back, leaning against the corner, leg draped across the cushion, long and comfortable. "Green," he says. "My turn. What is the weirdest thing you totally hate? Like weird enough you could not reveal this to anyone or they'd never let you live it down?"

"You make a strong case for telling you," I say.

"It's the rules," he says. "Bet you can't resist the *rules*."

I suppress a grin. Because he's right. With the notable exception of all of our back-and-forth sabotage this summer, I am a rule-follower. Particularly if those rules present a challenge. "Nemo," I say.

He blinks at me.

"The little fish from *Finding Nemo*."

His jaw drops. "*Nemo*? Bite your tongue. Nemo is fucking adorable."

"He's so annoying; literally every time he speaks, I think of all the different ways I would like to cook him."

Reid sits up. "Get out."

"I will not."

"Nemo, oh man, that's too much. You were right; you should have lied, no one will ever be capable of loving you after that."

He's laughing really hard and I'm laughing really hard because I know that is the most heartless thing I have ever actually vocalized.

My stomach is starting to hurt from all the laughing, and if we haven't woken someone up by now, it's a freaking miracle. "Now you know my deepest secret, Reid Yamada," I say.

He's wiping actual tears from his eyes. "Okay, ask me one of mine. Make it good; that one was worth a *lot* of information. *Nemo*."

"Oh man, my last question. So much pressure. I could ask your most embarrassing moment. What superpower you would have. How many people you've kissed . . . yes, okay that's the one." Tiredness is setting in. Making me bold. "How many girls have you kissed?"

Reid's eyes start to sparkle. He opens his mouth, then pauses. "Well. Wait. How many people or how many girls?"

"Uh," I say. "Either. Both. Can I . . . can I ask both?"

He says, "For anything less than Nemo, I would have said no. But okay, yeah. I've kissed three girls."

It is completely ridiculous that the emotion flaring up in my chest is absolutely jealousy. Get it together, self, this is two in the morning talking. We are not jealous of girls who have had their tongues in Reid Yamada's mouth.

We definitely, DEFINITELY are not.

I swallow hard.

"Five people, total."

"Wow, okay," I say.

"One guy. Last person I dated was nonbinary."

"I didn't realize you were bi, I don't think. Is that the right word?"

"I mean, yeah, it can be. There's . . . a lot of words that can be the right one. I don't know, I kind of just like queer, honestly? And how would you know, anyway. Not like I introduce myself with it. *Hi, I'm Reid Yamada. Ask me how I do or do not experience sexual attraction and also the genders of people I would like to bang.*"

I'm laughing again, which I guess is the order of the night. "Fair. Your question."

He's leaning close now, and I think maybe it's a conscious choice.

I think maybe I have been moving toward him, too, and maybe I wasn't as unaware of it as I should have been.

As though there's any *should* involved in anything here.

He says, "Tell me about the best kiss of your life."

"Form of a question."

"We playing *Jeopardy* now?"

I lock eyes with him. We're so close, and the fire is bright in the dark. And I guess I never had occasion to realize how many little shades of brown were peppered through his. Dark as polished wood in some places, light as amber in others. I can't breathe for a second. And I think maybe he will just kiss me.

It's the craziest thing.

But I think . . . I think maybe he will, and maybe, because I have slipped into some alternate timeline over the course of the night, I'll kiss him back, and so I stop the whole thing from starting and say, "Jackson Rhodes."

Reid gives me that utterly destructive half-smile. "Do tell."

"Tenth grade. It wasn't any place special or anything. Not like we made out in the rain and I could check an item off my bucket list. It was at my friend's house. I'd kind of been flirting with him for a couple months and he'd been flirting back, probably harder than I'd been, honestly. So it was just a few of us watching some old movie in Em's shitty basement. Something old and super, like, violent or depressing, too. *Fight Club*? *Donnie Darko*? It might have been *Donnie Darko*."

"Oh man, I hate that movie."

"Because it's a terrible movie."

"Unlike *Finding Nemo*."

145

I flip him off and he rewards me with this single bark of a laugh. High-pitched in the way that anything borne of surprise comes out a little high-pitched.

"*Anyway*," I say, "Em had gone upstairs to make a frozen pizza, and a couple people were leaving. The other two had gone outside to smoke."

"You remember this really well."

"Bear trap," I say, tapping my head. "And yeah, it was definitely *Donnie Darko* because that terrifying rabbit thing showed up onscreen and I remember saying, *This guy is freaking horrifying, I hate this movie,* and he just kind of slid over so my head was on his shoulder, and I thought his deodorant smelled really, really good. And he looked down at me and said, *Have you considered not looking at the screen?* And I said, *That thought had crossed my mind, yeah.* And he was so nervous, like I could actually hear his heart going crazy, when he kissed me." I lean my head back against the couch. "It was his hands that did it. A kiss can't be great if you don't know what to do with your hands."

"Oh, I know," says Reid.

"God, I'd forgotten how amazing he was with his tongue, too."

"Okay," says Reid.

I glance over at him. "You alright?"

"Just tired," he says.

"I thought you were usually out here for like two hou—"

"Yeah, just. Challenge tomorrow and everything. Tiredness kind of just hit me all at once." His voice is a little shaky.

"You sure you're—"

He stands and I blink. "I'm glad we did this."

I smooth my hands over the couch and stand with him. "Me, uh, me too."

He runs his tongue over his bottom lip and rakes his hand back through his hair. "I'll see you tomorrow? Or. Today, I guess."

"Yeah," I say. "Yeah, okay." And it feels bizarrely abrupt and I am unsettled when I head up the stairs to go to bed.

The way this got cut short is only one of the reasons.

# CHAPTER EIGHTEEN

In the cold light of day, under the buzzing kitchen fluo-rescents, I am . . . kind of uncomfortable. Just standing there next to Reid, neither of us quite looking at each other. In the dark, it didn't seem like we were revealing a whole lot, just seemed like we were talking. Having a totally average interaction.

In the morning, it feels like he told me his deepest fear was losing people and I told him about the specific skill level of a boy's tongue, and he told me he was queer, and maybe we almost kissed.

But, eight hours later, that feels kind of foggy, too. Like I could have just completely made it up. I don't know. All I know is, he looks as uncomfortable as I feel, and I'm really hoping he's not regretting anything.

Thank the lord the only thing either of us has to regret is the exchange of information.

Dr. Freeman, thankfully, releases us from this contest of muteness by saying, "This week, we will only have one challenge. Conducted in two parts."

I don't know if that's higher pressure or lower. I'm tensing up either way.

She continues, "This challenge is long-form and will be started today, concluded tomorrow evening. Teams, send one member to the judges' table."

Reid tips his chin at me and goes. The length of his legs compared to mine, a quick calculation says, means it is less work for him to do it. He walks back to me with an envelope in his hand, and I want to open it, and I don't want to open it.

"Open your envelopes," Dr. Freeman instructs.

Well, that settles that.

"Oh, damn," says Andrew at something in the contents, and I purse my lips, eyelids dropping in annoyance.

Dr. Freeman ignores him. "In them, you will find a detailed menu. Following that will be a client profile. Each of you has received, at random, a client with some sort of dietary restriction or preference. They have all been determined to be of equal difficulty level or negligible difference, so I expect no complaints. Behind those things, you have each been provided money, with which you will shop today for your ingredients. You will stock them in the fridge in the packaging that will be provided to you, and let me make this clear: there will be *no tampering with anyone's ingredients*. One of your judges will be available from one-thirty p.m. on to personally check ingredients to ensure that no tampering occurs. Is that clear?"

I am standing at attention, nervous as hell that maybe somehow they know. Which is kind of nonsense; maybe they're just paranoid. Or have had people pull crap in previous years. Doesn't really matter, I'm totally concerned anyway and I'm sure it shows on my face. When I glance up, Reid's mouth is twitching. Suddenly, I'm relaxed.

"Yes, ma'am," we all say, and I wonder just how this would have gone were Reid and I not allied.

Maybe we both would have been honest about it.

I almost laugh out loud at that.

"There is an open-air market just up the road. A map has been provided for you on the back of your client sheet. Let me also make clear that that is a thing you will want to utilize. If you're the only team using grocery store ingredients and everyone else has purchased them fresh, we *will* notice."

Another chorus of "Yes, ma'am"s.

"You have until three-thirty p.m. to be back here with your collections. One minute later and there will be no one in the kitchens and your team will have been eliminated."

I stand tall and take a deep breath. That's only intimidating because of the finality of it. The challenge itself is simple: buy groceries. And don't take like a BILLION hours to do it.

"Begin," says Dr. Freeman and I turn to Reid.

"Hand me the menu."

He raises his eyebrows. "Yes ma'am."

"What's our restriction?"

"Walk and talk," he says, and we leave the kitchen. "Looks like it's a gluten thing."

"Okay, that seems doable."

"Yeah. How long's that menu? Do we have to do the whole thing?"

I laugh. "No way. We're gonna have to pick something to cater to the client. Wow, there are even ingredients listed for the meals. Dude, they gave us *recipes*. This doesn't seem bad. Like . . . this is practically a free day."

"Seems like it," says Reid, but his voice is coated in suspicion.

We study the menu as we walk—me with eyes on the paper, him on a phone, cross-checking ingredients for gluten.

We hop a bus to the open-air market several miles outside Savannah, and everything seems pretty easy.

Until it isn't.

And the moment we realize that this day is going to be a challenge is this: we lay eyes on the price of the first shank of lamb.

"Reid," I say.

"Oh, I noticed."

"Should we—count what we have again."

Reid purses his lips, and there's this furrow in his brow again, the adorable one, not that the adorableness of that brow crease matters overmuch right now. "I've counted it four times, *mon petit chou*."

"If we buy that lamb, there's no way we can possibly afford all the spices for it. Or the side dish! We can barely afford the potatoes, let alone fresh cream for them. Oh no. We're going to lose, we're going to lose. Switch. Switch the dish."

"Every other main dish has gluten in it."

My eyes go wide. "That can't be right." I go over the list. It turns out that, in fact, it can.

"Shit," he says, laughing. "What do you want to bet everyone is freaking out about exactly this, exactly now? I bet all this minimal cash in our envelope with this fancy-ass menu is designed to be impossible."

My eyes widen. "Everyone had only one option. And not enough money to make it."

Reid grits his teeth and kind of shakes his head, smiling. *"This is practically a free day."*

"Shut up," I say and I shove him in the shoulder.

Reid grabs his shoulder and fake-winces. "No violence against your competitors," he says.

"You're not my competitor, slick, you're my teammate."

"Touché."

"Well," I say, squaring my shoulders, "let's conquer this Everest."

We wind through the market, trying to figure out what we can substitute, what can stay the same, if we can maybe cut down on the lamb shank a little if we make up for it in the potato side dish. What spices we might only need half of, or that have a cheaper substitute somewhere. We hit the jackpot at one vendor who has a ton of herbs at like 60 percent off because they're all gonna go bad in like a day.

It's not too terrible.

What makes it not-terrible, I absolutely hate to admit, is that I am spending this stressful day with Reid. Reid glances down at the herb choices and asks my opinion before picking one up. He says, "You go find the best cream here and I'll find something minty to make this work, meet in the middle?" And he doesn't check what I bought before he accepts it as a good choice.

I am completely blindsided by it all.

When the sun blazes over us and it's midday, time starting to wind down, we head to Tybee Beach, like a half mile away, to pick up lunch. We'll head back after and have like a couple hours to spare.

We stop by this little seafood hole-in-the-wall, and he gets something crawfish and I get shrimp and grits. When in Rome.

We don't eat inside; instead we take all our stuff to the beach, and we eat with our toes in the water. It's kind of loud, but not deafening. Calm waves lapping at our ankles.

"I don't get it," I say. Then, "Oh my god, these grits are incredible."

"What don't you get? The grits?" He smirks and I roll my eyes.

"You," I say.

Reid raises an eyebrow. "The question stands."

"Just . . ." I look out over the water. "You. Today it's like nothing but respect when it's been all assholery and you checking to make sure I'm slicing my carrots thin enough before you'll allow them to go into our dish. And arrogance which—I hate this but I guess you've earned the right to it; you're better than all of us. It's throwing me off."

Reid peers at me then, and I set my spoon back in its bowl. I look right back.

"Do you think you're not as good as me?"

I blush. I don't know why I'm blushing. But my face is red-hot and my stomach twists like a dishrag—hard and uncomfortable and I don't . . . I don't want to answer.

He keeps looking, and I think maybe he'll wait forever for me to answer. I think maybe I'll wait longer.

He doesn't. He says, "Do you think *I* think you're not as good as me?"

I actually laugh. "Of course you think that."

Reid scoffs.

I say, "Please. You think you're God."

"I *do not* think I'm God."

I say, "Okay," with as much sarcasm as I can muster and look back over the ocean. It looks . . . endless.

"And I never thought I was better than you."

I snort.

"I'm serious; hey, look at me."

I do.

He's looking at me like he *knows* me. His face is this weird blend of fallen and intense. Like he's sad, in one turn. But in the next, it's like he sees a thousand things about me that no one else on this beach does, and I can't breathe.

"If you . . . Jesus, if I made you feel like that, I'm sorry."

My throat constricts harder.

"You think I'd pick my enemy number one if I didn't think she was *really fucking good*? You're good, Lane. You're . . . great. If you weren't, I would have dropped this whole thing we had between us."

"Thing . . . thing we had between us?" My mind snags on the past tense, and I don't want it to.

"The whole rivalry stuff, yeah. I would have quit after you had your revenge. I'm glad we're paired, Lane. Because you're *good*."

My mouth drops and I glance down at the sand, at the half-inch of space between my thumb and his fingers, and everything feels dangerous, suddenly.

Feels like that ocean is closing us in, and my focus is just zeroing in on him breathing. I can feel him looking at me. Smell the light, clean deodorant he uses, and the spicy crawfish beside him, hear him breathing.

I glance up at him and he brushes this stray strand of lavender hair—it's faded to that by now—away from my forehead.

I jump up. Like, leap from my butt to my feet. "We should probably go."

"Uh," he says. "Yeah." He chokes a little and says, "Yeah. We should. Gotta get all this back before we get DQ'd. Yeah." He stands. "Let's go."

We do.

I'm still savoring the grits.

"Have you never had those before?" he says.

"Nope."

"What a tragedy."

I shrug. "I bet there's things you've never tried."

"Ghost peppers. Mustard-based barbecue. Weed brownies."

I laugh loud. "Living in Colorado, even. Let's see. For me. Well, grits. Caviar. Macarons."

"You've never had *macarons*? Is the entirety of Montana *FARGO*?"

I sniff. Prim. "That's set in Minnesota."

"Well if they don't have macarons, they're the same. Dead to me."

I smirk and shove him.

He grabs my hand, presses it there for a split-second before he drops it.

Normal.

Regular.

Neutral.

Everything is perfectly, *regularly* middle-of-the-road. And that is why my heart rate doesn't slow the whole trip back.

# CHAPTER NINETEEN

I leave for breakfast a little earlier than Riya; she's spending eight hundred years on her makeup this morning.

And when I open the door to my dorm room, I almost step in something.

Something that very much should not be stepped in—not because it's disgusting and you wouldn't want it on your foot, but because it would be an utter sin to ruin it with a misplaced body part.

It's this plate, stacked with macarons. Every color that exists. Bright yellow and pink and teal and brown, oh my *gosh*.

I bend down and pick it up, reverently.

There's a little note on top, hastily written and stained with almond flour and dye. It says *fix your life, princess.*

I'm blushing from my head down to my toes; even my feet feel legitimately hot.

I just stare at the plate, trying to catalogue all the colors and the work that must have gone into this last night. It's a heck of a lot more than two hours' insomnia.

Riya's voice pops up behind me: "Oh. My god."

"It's nothing," I say.

"Yeah. Nothing that's going in my face immediately."

I pick a little pink one with green in the middle and take a bite. It's amazing. Strawberry lime—light and dense all at once; I feel like I can literally taste the color.

"Holy crap," I say.

Riya is eating a yellow one. "Is this . . . who made you these?"

I swallow hard. "Definitely not Reid Yamada."

Riya laughs until she chokes on a macaron.

Good.

Reid is smiling like the devil when I find him in the kitchen, weighing a skillet in his hand.

"Lane."

"Thank you," I say.

"It wasn't really a compliment but sure, you can take it that way."

I roll my eyes. "I meant for the—the macarons."

He says, "Oh, those couldn't have been from me." And winks.

The challenge starts, and I'm pink all over once again.

The cooking itself isn't too bad. Everyone but me is a little demoralized this morning, and I wonder who compromised on what, who's cooking what. We're a little short on time, but it's nothing too crazy. This challenge was about prioritizing. And *actually* cooking. Actual skills.

Afterward, Reid shoulder-bumps me and says, "What are you doing after this?"

"I have a very busy itinerary of Netflix and iced tea planned for my room later, packed schedule honestly."

"Wow. What are the odds that you and I have the exact same afternoon going here?"

"What *are* the odds."

"Let me present a counter-offer," he says, shoving his hands down into his pockets as we walk across the grass.

"Go for it," I say.

"Come watch Netflix and have iced tea in *my* room."

I stop walking and my eyebrows shoot up.

"Shit," he says, and he throws his hands in the air. He's already laughing.

"Are you asking me to Netflix and chill with you, Yamada?"

"Again with the last name. No, I swear I am asking you to literally Netflix and literally chill and you should literally bring up some literal iced tea. From the literal cafeteria."

"I think . . . okay, I could literally be down with that."

His mouth tips up. "Well, you could . . . you could be figuratively down with that."

"You are such an ass," I say. But I follow it up with, "Ten minutes?"

"It's a date." For the first time ever, I see Reid Yamada blush. He doesn't stammer when he corrects himself; he looks cool and collected, all but for that red in his cheeks. "An entirely platonic, Netflix and iced tea two-people gathering."

I'm smiling and it's ridiculous. I have no idea if Em would be thrilled or smug or completely at a loss. Maybe she would think it was un-feminist of me. To be hanging out with Reid, who's been such a jerk to me all summer.

But well. I don't think I care.

I, of course, shoot her a text about it which she probably won't get to until tonight, complete with the most panicked emojis I can find and a shot of the macarons from this morning. I caption that picture: *HELP?!?!?!?!?*

Then I head into the cafeteria and Reid takes the stairs to his room. Probably cleaning up like, underwear or whatever. Now I'm blushing. About Reid's underwear. Oh my lord, what is happening to me?

I am grateful, suddenly, that there are two beds in there; thank you, Reid's dearly departed roommate, because that's the only thing that makes this not-weird. I don't know. Maybe it's weird anyway.

I feel weird.

I feel good.

. . . I feel weird.

I snag a couple bottled teas and run upstairs, knock on his door.

"That was definitely less than ten minutes," he says when he opens it.

"I'm nothing if not prompt."

He lets me pass and I toss him the tea, which he catches out of the air. Then he plops down on his giant be—"Hey," I say. "There's . . . there's two beds in here. I thought there were two beds in here."

"Oh." He looks down at the very singular monstrosity he's lying on and then says, "How would you kn—oh right. The cellular privacy invasion heist thing. Well. There were two but I pushed them together. I'm kind of a sprawler when I sleep."

My throat is really dry all of a sudden even though it's the middle of the day, even though he's not, like, making a move. My heart is beating right up into that dry throat and what even is breathing?

"I can push them apart if that would make you feel better?" he says. "It's not a big deal. I'll push them apart."

"No," I say when I find my words. "No, it's whatever. You don't need to rearrange your whole room for me. It's fine." I plop down onto his mattress before he has the chance to split them.

"Okay. You sure?"

"I'm sure. What's on Netflix?"

Reid shrugs and lies back against the headboard, one arm stretched behind his head, the other working the remote. He flips through a few things 'til he hits disaster movies and I say, "Yesssssss."

"Really?" he says. He's grinning.

"Huge disaster movie nerd."

"Ha. Me too."

There's an uncomfortable niggling in my chest, a flutter in my stomach, and I stare hard at the TV. "Pick that one."

"Which one, Captain Obvious?"

"The frog one."

"God, that looks ridiculous," he says. He's laughing when he hits play.

The opening scene is one of those highly dramatic evolution sequences that like starts as one cell, and then splits into more, and then eventually you have in front of you this wriggling mass of tadpoles set to extremely ominous music, and the opening credits end zooming out on a frog's eye.

The title is punctuated with the most threatening croak I have ever heard.

"I think you mean amazing," I say.

"Not mutually exclusive, Purple Rain."

"Purple Rain."

"It's song."

"I know it's a song but it's not a nickname and you know it."

He arches an eyebrow and looks down at me. Stretches his arm when he shifts so it's resting on one of the big ridges in the headboard. I'm not squished by any means but I am struck with how much space he tends to take up. Just moving, just the way he holds himself. I'm struck by the way I can actually feel it when he trains his eyes on me. "You didn't object to Purple Haze."

"Well," I say, "that feels like less of a stretch than Purple Rain."

He laughs. "'Purple Rain' is by Prince. His signature color was purple; if anything, that's a nicknamed-squared."

I just look at him, totally nonplussed, and turn toward the TV. There's a schoolteacher who looks like she's from the sixties even though this movie came out like two years ago. I say, still looking at the screen, "Did you Google purple nicknames just for this occasion?"

I'm deadpanning it. It's a joke, which is why I'm jolted enough to actually stop and look at him when he says, "Yeah," with this single almost self-deprecating laugh.

*Almost.* Because nothing Reid ever says really totally gets there. Cocky lives in his skin cells.

"Wait, are you serious?"

"I was running low on material."

I try not to smile and he looks down at exactly the moment I am failing the hardest and smiling the most.

He doesn't say anything. He just looks back at the screen, lets one corner of his mouth curl, and watches the frogs devour every living thing on the planet.

"Tell me your favorite food," he says.

"Grilled cheese."

He doesn't skip a beat. "With provolone."

"Yes. You asshole."

That corner of his mouth reaches higher.

"What's yours?" I say, and I'm on fire again, because talking about our favorite foods feels like something way more intimate than it should. It's the thing each of us is most passionate about. It's like asking a reader their favorite book. Asking a fighter their favorite move. It's a soul-level question.

And I am desperate to know the answer.

This slow smile spreads over his face and he says, "Nabe, for sure."

"I've never had that."

"Yeah, well, you're not Japanese. And nabe isn't like, *American* Japanese food; it's the real deal."

"Tell me about it."

"It's something my dad makes in the winter. He got it from his mom, who brought it over here from Japan, and I basically beg for it all the time. Mom doesn't really cook. And she's white and from Texas so if she does it's like fried chicken and sweet tea. Season shit with a little salt."

I spit out a laugh.

"So basically nabe is—well. Wait. What if I showed you?"

I shift on the bed so I'm facing him. Cross-legged and small. The way he's twisted, looking down at me, it's *almost like* I'm right there, like he has his arm around me.

Stop.

*Stop, self.*

"You want to cook for me again? After all that labor over the macarons?"

He says, "Maybe I just wanted some myself and made too many. You got the excess."

I can't believe I'm just now noticing the dark circles under his eyes. The slight sleep-crazed note in his voice that comes from pulling an all-nighter.

"Take a thank-you."

He pauses. Then says, kind of quiet, "You're welcome."

I glance down at the bedspread. Smooth my fingers over it. "Can you make nabe in here?"

"No. Not even a little bit."

"Damn," I say.

His eyes spark. "Kitchen's open."

I lock eyes with him, and he looks like the incarnation of mischief. Like he's not asking me to go hang out in a teaching kitchen where we've spent way too much time over the summer, sweating in the heat while he makes me food. Like he's asking me to do something illegal.

I say, "Okay."

# CHAPTER TWENTY

They leave the kitchen locked, but let us reserve it if we want. For practice. Reid has to run over to their offices and pick up a key card, sign up to use it for a couple hours, but he runs back and I meet him at the kitchen a few minutes later.

He slides the key card and pushes open the door.

"Holding open the door for a girl; who even are you, and what have you done with Reid?"

"Please, I am the poster boy for chivalry."

I snort and head inside.

"It's weird," I say.

Reid raises an eyebrow and breezes past me into the kitchen. "What?"

"Being in here without the judges. I feel like I should be standing there sweating while a clock counts down."

"Have you never used this room to practice?"

"Have you?"

"I spend a solid half my time in here."

I smirk. "The time you're not spending running or reading about magic in the middle of the night."

Reid's face isn't turned toward me, but I see the grin when he dips down into one of the drawers and pulls out a few knives, a couple cutting boards. "Yeah. I mean obviously *that's* what I came here for."

"I haven't been in here at all, except when we're assigned."

"Slacker," he says. He ties an apron around his neck, his lower back, and my eyes are sliding toward the knots. Because *aprons* are sexy. Aprons.

"Some of us don't need all that practice to win," I say, looking at my nails.

"You say that now," he says. "Wait until this nabe knocks you on your ass."

I grin.

"You gonna help me out or?"

I narrow my eyes because he's *so polite, so charming.* Then say, "What did you need?"

"Get me some soy. And mirin. Sake if it's back there."

"What else?"

"Cabbage. Naganegi."

I blink and he goes to the fridge and pulls out some ground chicken and a few other things I can't see through his arms.

"Naganegi?" I say.

"Yeah. I don't need much."

"Okay but I have no idea what it is."

Reid looks right at me then, furrow in his brow, and laughs. "Oh. Right. Shit." He laughs. He looks so *relaxed* right now, I'm completely thrown off. "It's like…it's like this super long skinny onion? White? And it's—no, you know what; forget that. I'll get it when I get the mushrooms."

I nod and head back to get some ingredients. It doesn't take me long to find them, with the exception of the naga-negi, which I am glad Reid has released me from.

I head back into the kitchen and Reid passes me. He's completely focused on the task at hand.

He comes back and he has those onions, what looks like some tofu. Carrots. Just . . . a veritable shit ton of stuff.

"Are you going to use every single ingredient in the kitchen?"

"Yes."

He pauses before his army of cutting boards, examines everything. Then runs to the fridge and comes back with some pork and shell-on shrimp.

"Okay. You ready to get your hands dirty?"

"Always," I say, and then my face heats, but he's probably not thinking of that as a totally filthy reply because he's probably thinking about food, oh my lord, think about food.

"Pick a vegetable. Start chopping."

"How?" I say.

"Nabe's a stew. Some people call it nabemono, which is just literally 'hot pot stuff.' So. It doesn't matter how you chop it, dumplin'."

I groan and his eyes actually sparkle, but I get to chopping everything. It turns out Reid was lying when he said it didn't matter how I chopped it—mine is all brisk, efficient, and I move through everything twice as fast as he does, but by the time he finishes a carrot, it's a work of art. All his stuff is carved into like flowers and stars with way too much detail to be eaten.

"Show-off."

"Nah, this is me slacking." He winks.

"You trying to scare me?" I say, setting down my knife. All my stuff is done.

"I'm trying to impress you."

He says it like nothing, like it's not loaded. Like that's a boring, neutral sentence that won't lodge my heart somewhere in the neighborhood of my throat. I say somehow, "And why would you ever consider trying to do such a thing?"

Reid doesn't answer. He just slides his knife slowly and methodically through the center of a carrot and arches his eyebrow at me. Even more slowly. More methodically.

I blush.

The carrot falls apart into this beautiful spray of flowers.

Reid surveys what he has and ducks. Starts searching through doors for something, and I don't know what. I don't know how to vocalize my question because I'm stuck on that eyebrow raise. That *You know exactly why, Lane* look that has my heart racing so fast I can't think over it.

"Dammit, there's no way they're gonna have a—oh hey!" He emerges from deep within a pot/pan/kettle/ whatever door with a huge, cheesy grin on his face and says, "They do have a donabe!"

I give him a thumbs-up even though I do not understand the significance of the statement, but it seems important.

"Clay pot," he says. "You cook shit in it."

"Ah."

"Usually we'd do this over a flame tableside, but we have no table. So. Gas stovetop it is. This thing is giant but you typically make this for a lot of people, so I hope you are *completely starving*."

"I haven't eaten for four days just saving up for this."

"Prepared *and* psychic; helpful." He gets the broth boiling and then dumps like everything in it.

"So now we wait."

I lean back against one of the countertops and he walks over to me, then leans up against it, too. Arms folded over his chest. Easy. Chill. Relaxed.

"So I have a question," I say.

He glances down at me out of the corner of his eye. When he shifts, his hip brushes against mine and my fingers tighten on the counter. I can see every muscle tic through that shirt. Smell his deodorant this close, even though the nabe is starting to smell like something already.

"Shoot."

This has been bothering me for a few days and I don't know why I feel like now is the time to ask it. But I blurt out, "The other night. The insomnia talk."

"Yeah."

"Why did you leave like that?"

I can see his Adam's apple move when he swallows. His jaw must be carved from actual stone. Good lord.

I bet I'm bright pink. I'm sure I am because that's what happens when you stare at boys' throats and jaws for this long, like a sex-crazed maniac.

"Well," he says. His voice is smooth but he won't look at me. Even though I'm sure he feels me looking at him. "I, uh. I was thinking that I wanted to kiss you."

The boiling water, the buzz of the fluorescents, everything fades to white noise.

His hand goes to the back of his neck. "And I'm pretty damn sure you didn't want to kiss me. Don't. Didn't. Both tenses. So I left."

I blink down at the floor. The world has tilted to a new axis and I need to figure out how to balance on it. Reid. Wanted to kiss me.

Reid wanted to kiss me.

Reid. Wanted. To kiss me.

I am white-knuckling the counter.

And suddenly what I am is mad.

I'm *mad*. Like *always* now, apparently. "You wanted to *kiss me*?"

His eyebrows jump when he looks at me and says, "Yeah. Is that a problem?"

"YES," I say. "And let me tell you why, you asshole."

Reid's mouth flattens into a line.

The whole kitchen smells like divinity, and normally that would be enough to distract me from basically any emotion, but I'm vibrating. "Because you've been an ass to me since day one."

"I didn't want to kiss you on day one."

"No? Well how about day two? Or day three? Or day twenty-seven? Because I don't see anything that has changed here except we were forced to be on a team, but beyond that, it's been just complete Dicksville on your end."

He scoffs and leaves to turn the nabe down to simmer.

"That's rich coming from you," he says.

"No, you don't get to turn this all around on me."

"I'm *not*. I'm saying I'm not the only asshole around here. I'm *sorry I wanted to kiss you*, but this hasn't been me just picking on poor, helpless Carter from the first minute, and I'm not trying to say that I like, pulled your hair on the playground because I liked you. I did it because you were competition, and you played back *hard*."

"So that makes me the bad guy?"

"No, it makes you equally as assholey as me. We're the same, princess."

"Oh my god, with the princess stuff."

"Tell me you want me to stop saying it and I'll stop."

He takes a step toward me and anger is steaming off him, and it's rolling right off me in waves, and I'm pretty sure—yes, I think it's anger. I think I want to hit him. Right in that chest that's inches away from me. Knock him off balance.

I want him just completely off kilter because of me.

I move to hit him in the arm. Hard.

He catches my wrist.

Looks right down at me, locks me in place. The edge of the countertop is digging into my spine and heat is still pouring off me, but I'm not totally sure it comes from wanting to smash his face in.

I certainly don't think that's what he wants to do to mine.

He just looks. Mouth set. Jaw hard.

And I don't know what I'm doing until I've done it. Until I've already gotten up on my tiptoes and slipped a little at the top and landed this little nothing of a kiss on the very edge of his mouth.

I fall back to my ankles, still looking at him like I want to kill him.

His fingers are still wrapped around my wrist.

His lips part, just the tiniest bit.

Then his hands are both at my waist, fingers strong around it, and he's lifting me up on the counter. And he's kissing me.

It feels like we're fighting, feels like no one I've ever kissed.

Feels like I'll never be able to think straight again, and maybe I'm not interested in that anyway. I definitely can't think *now*, with Reid's tongue slipping between my teeth, his hips resting between my knees, at my thighs, teeth scraping over my lip.

One of my hands is sliding up into his hair and the other links in his belt loop, yanking him into me.

He loses his balance and I smile against his mouth. "Weak in the knees?" I say.

He looks down at me, just this side of predatory, and smirks when he laughs. "Sure." He kisses me again, deep and slow, and what the hell, what the hell are we doing? I don't care.

I don't care.

I'm too busy being breathless to care.

I reach around his back to untie the apron, and the rope gets caught for a second on his neck, the top loop, but I don't care.

It drops to the floor.

Then his hand is slipping up around the back of my neck, thumb grazing my throat and my ear and my jaw. His other hand is staying there, right at my hip, playing lazily over my skin.

I'm tugging him into me because I want to be pressed against him.

I can't believe I'm saying this.

He makes this almost desperate noise in the back of his throat. Reid Yamada. Desperate. Over me.

He tightens his fingers at my waist, and the ones on my neck curl in my hair, and I knock my head against the cabinet and he says, "SHIT I'm sorry," and I say, "It doesn't matter," even though to be honest it kind of matters—my head hurts. We make out until I take a half a second to breathe and say, "Oh. The nabe!"

Reid swallows hard, voice hoarse. "Yeah. Yeah, the nabe. What was I thinking cooking for you when we could have been doing this?"

"That you wanted to impress me."

Reid pulls back. He looks out of breath. Disheveled. Upside down. The way I feel. It's surreal. He finds the presence of mind to smirk and say, "Did it work?"

"You mean am I impressed?"

"Yeah."

"Jury's out," I say.

He laughs. Really hard.

"I mean, I haven't tried the nabe."

Reid leans back against the island in front of me, looks up at the ceiling, and blows out a breath.

"Yeah. Well. Let's, uh. God—sorry."

A smile curls my mouth and I slide off the counter. For once, I think maybe I actually look like the put together one.

I pick up the donabe with oven mitts, then set it down on another mitt, right in the middle of the floor between the judge's table and the kitchen.

"Bring bowls," I say.

It takes him way too long to bring them. Bowls, spoons. He sits cross-legged on the other side of the pot.

"Are we cool?" he says. His eyes are still half-glazed, his hair all messed up, and he wants me so badly to answer a certain way. I'm a little high on the power of all of it.

I'm a little high on Reid.

Kissing is great.

Making out is great.

It's all great.

"Wait until I taste this nabe," I say.

He gives me a completely nonplussed look.

"But," I say primly, filling my bowl, "outlook is good. You have above average knowledge of what to do with your hands."

Reid laughs.

I smile.

# CHAPTER TWENTY

I wake up panicking.

Just.

Panicking.

I know what Reid's mouth tastes like and oh my lord, Reid knows what *mine* tastes like, and let's be real, that's a lot to know about a person. It's TOO MUCH to know about a person.

I am just blinking up at the ceiling.

Blinking and blinking and blinking.

Riya is already up, in the shower, and when she comes out, wrapped in a towel, I blurt out, "Did you know Reid chews cinnamon gum?"

Riya blinks. "I . . . I did not."

"I hate cinnamon gum."

She doesn't say anything.

"Once, I chewed too much of it and it blistered my mouth. Can you believe that? Gum. Blistered my mouth!"

Riya says, "Carter."

I say, "Gum should be mint."

"Carter. Are you about to have a complete breakdown?"

"Wintergreen or spearmint, specifically. Peppermint burns my mouth, too."

Riya has her arms folded across her chest and she throws out, "Did Reid's cinnamon gum burn you?"

I say, "No, Reid's cinnamon-gum-flavored mouth burned me oh my god what did I do?"

My face is in my hands, which is a shame, because I miss Riya's facial expression when she makes the most strangled, surprised laugh sound. "Excuse me?"

I peek through my fingers. "I kissed Reid."

"Wait, I need to have clothes on. Wait." She snags a shirt and shorts and runs back into the bathroom in a change that probably sets some kind of world record for speed. "GO."

"Well. He made me food. More food. After the macarons."

Riya's eyes morph into actual hearts.

"And then I told him I hated him, basically, because how dare he want to kiss me, and then I kissed him."

"With tongue?"

"NO." I amend, "No. I didn't . . . I didn't use tongue when . . . when I kissed *him*."

Riya cackles. "So he kissed you. With tongue."

I can't not smile so I say, "On the kitchen counter."

"CARTER."

"I DON'T KNOW."

"Why do you look like you're in a complete panic?"

I shrug. "Because I'm not sure how to deal with this. We hate each other."

Riya says, "Yeah, obviously." Rolls her eyes.

"But now it's like, I don't know. I don't know what to do."

Riya smooths her hand over her bedspread. "For what it's worth, he's . . . he's liked you for a while."

I furrow my brow.

"He told Will. Like, weeks ago."

I squeal, "What? And you didn't tell me?" I throw a pillow at her and she catches it.

"Wasn't my secret to tell. It's just, I think he really does like you. Like *you*. Not just . . . making out with you in the kitchen. Not from what he said to Will."

"What did he say to Will?"

She says, "Can't tell you that. Just—he likes you. And you . . . I mean, it seems pretty clear you like him; you've basically been obsessed with him since you showed up here."

"I HAVEN'T BEEN—obsessed. With him." My voice gets smaller as the protest goes on because she's right.

I like him.

I've *been* liking him and I'm so mad about it, but I do.

I sigh heavily.

When it's time to go down for breakfast, Riya keeps her eyes on me. Probably wondering what I'm gonna do, if I'm gonna just break down right here or tackle Reid to the floor and make out with him right in the middle of the caf.

I don't do either of those things.

I walk in, get my tray. The cafeteria is pretty empty now, with just eight of us left.

Andrew, Addie, Reid, Will, Riya, Tess, her teammate, whom I have since learned is named Katie, and me.

I can't blend in; there's not enough bodies to get lost in the midst of. Reid looks at me from across the room, and I look back. He starts to smile.

I walk off.

I'm sitting by the river, throwing rocks into it. Thinking. Trying not to think. It's just all surprising and it's all a lot and I don't do well with things that are either. *Both* is really throwing me for a loop.

Seeing him in there was like a shot of lightning cracking through my sternum. Suddenly I was back in that kitchen, his hands on me, mouth doing these freaking magical things, bumping my head because the boy can kiss but he's a teenage boy and he's clumsy, and all these things that I am *terrified* to want.

I am terrified to want any of this.

Especially since it's all going to end anyway.

I was terrified to apply in the first place; Em had to sit beside me while I wrote the essay for hours, then actually click the mouse to get me to hit Send on the application.

I was terrified to open the letter.

Now I'm terrified to want to win, because wanting is just this side of hoping, and wanting things is stupid, because most things I want, I do not get, and that's been okay. It's been okay. And I want this. Dammit. I do.

I'm terrified to want Reid—this sharp, beautiful boy with wit that matches mine, who respects me in this weird way, enough to fight against me, enough to spend all summer thinking about me. Who like . . . trusts me and kisses me like I swear no one has *ever* kissed me, not even a boy in a basement watching *Donnie Darko*. I feel like . . . okay, it's a summer thing. And we're going to part ways and he's going to completely forget about me, but if I let myself fall, I won't forget. And it will just be all this crushing, stupid disappointment I could have avoided by never wanting him in the first place.

How was I so stupid?

Isn't wanting one impossible thing at a time enough?

I brush my hand over my pocket. I've had a text from Em waiting on *Read* for an hour; she's been grilling me about the macarons and the kiss and what's happening over here—didn't we hate Reid? But I don't even know how to answer. All of a sudden, everything just feels too big.

The grass rustles beside me and a shadow falls over it. I don't need to look to know it's Reid; I recognize what it feels like just existing in his periphery.

"How'd you find me?" I say.

"Lucky guess."

I look over at him.

He shrugs. "Okay. I checked the dorm, and then you weren't there, so I jogged the quad, and my next stop was the river."

I'm looking at the water when I say, "Where were you gonna go if I wasn't here?"

He says, "Kitchens. But I didn't have high hopes." It's quiet for a minute, then he says, "What are ya doing out here, Lane?"

"Nothing. Thinking."

"Nothing or thinking?"

"Freaking out," I say.

"Ah. Yeah I thought I recognized the panic." He shifts a little closer to me, and his voice is so gentle that it's a surprise. Like I have HANDLE WITH CARE stamped across my forehead. "Wanna elaborate or leave me in the dark?"

"I don't know how to elaborate."

"Is it . . ." He takes a deep breath. "Is it me?"

I don't say anything.

He says, "Okay. I can go."

"Don't go," I say. I don't know why; I thought I wanted him to.

He pauses. Looks at me. I can feel his gaze at the side of my face. "Then I'll stay." That quiet again. I don't know what to say. "I like you, princess," he says, and oh no, oh no, I guess I'm crying.

He doesn't ask me why, and I'm not sure if it's because he's one of those guys who's terrified of girls crying, but I don't think that's it.

Because he doesn't ask, but he slides his arm around my shoulders and pulls me over into him so my legs are draped across his lap and my head is resting between his neck and shoulder. I say, "This is embarrassing."

He says, "I could start crying if you want."

I hit him, and his hand darts up to press my wrist where it landed on his chest. "I don't know how to deal with this," I say.

"With what?" He says it, and his voice rumbles in my hair.

Reid is not my therapist. I'm not going to sit here, cradled against this guy I didn't even know I liked—well, didn't *acknowledge* I liked, until like yesterday—and go through my deepest, darkest psychological issues.

"I'm freaked out."

"What freaks you out?"

"You."

"Me?" He sounds surprised, and so I clarify.

"Not . . . not you. I'm not scared of you. I just like you and you're going to leave and I'm going to leave and then we like each other and we're both sad and we forget each other." *Or at least I'm sad. And I'm scared to want someone like you at all. This person who commands all the attention in any room, and who walks through the world like it will move for him if he needs it to. How does a person like that not just keep walking on and detach themselves from you? From everything. And how does a person like me get to want and possibly have someone like that?*

"Hey," he says. I feel the word vibrating from his chest out into my cheek and I pull back and look up. "I don't know what makes you think I'm going to just . . . forget you when I walk out of here. Or like, I don't know, is there a rule that says once this is over, everything that happened here is, too? What happens in Savannah stays in Savannah?"

I furrow my brow. I'm not crying now, which is good. It affords me the opportunity to speak. "No." I don't take as much advantage of that opportunity as perhaps I should.

"What if we just did whatever it is we're gonna do here? And then just . . . let the rest of everything happen— whatever that is? However it wants to happen."

I almost laugh, because it does *not* work that way for me. Maybe for him, who has made cocky and confident and go-with-the-flow a part of his soul, basically. But apart from at the skillet, I don't remember the last time I let things just happen. Because my brain is mapping out all the reasons it won't and how to prepare for those even-tualities, which sometimes feel more like certainties. "I thought you said you had anxiety," I say.

"*Social.*"

"Well this is *social.*"

"You're welcome to join me in the aftermath. I have a great two to four a.m. planned in which I will freak the hell out about all of it. And to try to decide if pulling you onto my lap was too much, and if I made you nervous and oh god oh god did I make her cry? Is that okay? And what if I like her more than she likes me, and oh no why did I admit that during my whole anxiety rant, great, I probably chased her away, way to go, self."

I blink.

"Standing invitation," he says. "But I'm fine right now."

"I don't get how you can do that," I say.

"And I don't get how you can just deal with all of this right here right now and not be kept up with thoughts about it later. Maybe we can trade brains for the night, see how that goes."

I smile and he slips his fingers over my jaw, laces them over my ear.

"I don't know what you want," he says. "But I know what I want."

"And what is that?" I say.

"Come on, Lane," he says.

I know what he wants. And I know . . . I know what I want, too. It's just that it's terrifying; all of this is terrifying. It's terrifying to want.

But it's so exhausting not to.

I don't look away from him. Sitting here on his lap like we're a couple, like this is comfortable and normal. The fear of all of that sinks down into my gut, past all my bones and organs and the intangible invisible parts of me floating around in there somewhere, but what if. What if I just . . . let things happen how they're going to happen? For once.

What if I at least *tried*?

I say, "I know."

He says, "You know what I want, or you know what you want?"

I'm shaking, and I wonder if he can feel it? Of course he can feel it. "Both," I say. I don't know how to want it, but I know that I *do*.

His fingers are in my hair.

He moves in slow, hands sliding over my cheek. Mine slide up under the hem of his shirt and his reaction is small, almost imperceptible, but it's there in this split-second flash of teeth on his bottom lip. He says, "Can I kiss you?" against my mouth.

I say, "You've already kissed me."

"Can I do it again?"

I kiss him.

It's slow. Like we are figuring each other out. Figuring out how exactly to kiss each other and touch each other and how to be this thing we didn't think we were but we are now. He kisses me like we have nothing but time, like the summer isn't running on a ticking clock. I kiss *him* with tongue, which Riya would be happy about, and I think I don't mind so much that we know what each other's mouths taste like.

Because now I know what his hipbones feel like against my legs, and what his fingers feel like trailing over my spine.

I know a lot of things about Reid that no one else here knows.

And I like it.

I'm not panicking for five seconds, because I *like it*.

# CHAPTER TWENTY-TWO

The next challenge comes, and this time it's a speed round. It's kind of a shock to the system after the last long-form thing, but we have thirty minutes to throw together a dessert that would be equally pleasing to a crowd of wealthy adults and to their toddler children. And for the first time, Reid and I aren't working against each other.

Reid is power-walking from one end of the kitchen to the back with the ingredients like he owns it, and I am in charge of whipping this chocolate into submission while Reid takes care of the pomegranate, and for once—for *once*—I don't feel like I shouldn't be here. The chocolate bubbles perfectly and melts into this total silk, and the tiny cakes we have in the oven puff exactly right. Everything, *everything* goes exactly right. Reid catches my eye when he comes back from picking up some powdered sugar and winks. My whole body flashes hot, and to be honest, it's done that basically every time he's looked at me in this kitchen, but for a thousand different reasons.

The thing I feel, mixing these pomegranate seeds in with this chocolate, is confident.

I feel like I am allowed to be here, in this kitchen.

I feel like I *deserve* to be here.

I feel like maybe I could win.

We set out our dishes and judging goes well, like we both knew it would, and we head out of the kitchen.

"Doing a little charity work?" I hear from behind us.

"What?" I say.

Andrew jogs up and gets in front of Reid. He cocks his head at me. "Helping those less fortunate, eh, Yamada?"

Reid narrows his eyes. He doesn't stop walking, and Andrew doesn't move so Reid winds up shoulder-bumping him and Andrew makes this noise like it just hurt so much. He's way bigger than Reid; I doubt it even stung. But Reid is sharp. Maybe his shoulders are too.

I tighten my fingers in Reid's and Andrew says, "What the hell?"

Reid says, "We have somewhere to be."

Andrew says, "Yeah, I bet you do." He smirks and it's gross and I don't even know what he's trying to do. "Nice of you to put so much time into this little thing, though. She could use the help. In and out of the kitchen."

I stop short. "What is your *problem*, Andrew?"

Andrew smiles with his teeth. "My problem is you shouldn't be here."

Reid gets a little taller, his hand on mine a little tighter. But he doesn't speak. He waits for me to, because he knows I'm going to. I've spent the whole summer fighting against him; I can take this asshole.

"Scared?"

Andrew laughs. "Hell no."

"Then why are you wasting your breath on me?"

He raises his eyebrows. "Maybe I'm pissed I've seen a bunch of guys go home while you stay. There's a billion more dude chefs than girls and this program is like 50/50. Everyone knows that's like affirmative action or whatever."

I blink.

"I was on a team with you. You spend half your time screwing up. Maybe I'm pissed we're this close to the end and you're gonna stay another week because you got lucky enough to be paired with Yamada here. It's bullshit."

Something twists in my chest and I just deflate.

I don't want to.

I want to be one of those people who has witty retorts that stick with people months after you fire them back. I've been that person, with Reid. Whip sharp, firing off these little zingers without a thought. But Andrew doesn't make my veins feel like lightning is crackling through them. Andrew makes them feel like sludge.

I deserve to be here.

I *deserve* to be here.

Reid says, voice so low I can barely hear him over the sound of my own brain, "Turn the hell around before I kick your ass."

Andrew has the nerve to look surprised. He says, "Whoa, Mr. Miyagi, we don't need to resort to violence."

Reid says, "Yeah?" And takes a step forward.

Andrew's face moves from surprised to nervous.

"Shut your mouth," I say to Andrew because I have somehow found my words.

Andrew doesn't look at me. He looks at Reid, and Reid's hand—fingers tapping his thigh like they're itching to curl.

185

"I don't want to start something," Andrew says.

Reid says, "You already did. So how about you head the hell out before I finish it?"

Andrew just scoffs and takes a look at me, raises his eyebrow like the point stands. And leaves.

I'm furious.

I'm furious and I'm suddenly so tired because that balloon expanding in my chest back in the kitchen? Popped. Just like that.

I can't stop thinking *Charity case, charity case, charity case.*

Am I lucky I was paired with Reid? Is that true? Like the kid who can barely sink a two-pointer who gets picked for the varsity basketball player's team in P.E.?

Five minutes ago, I would have said no, and now I'm not sure.

Solid foundation of confidence here.

Reid says, "That guy's an asshole," and we walk.

Past the quad, through the doors, all the way up to his room.

I close the door behind us and slide down it to the floor, hands linked across my shins. "Yeah."

"Carter. You know what he said is bullshit, right?"

I glance up at him. "Yeah," I say, but there's no resolve behind it. "Yeah. Of course—of course it is."

"He said that shit because he's scared of you. He knows you're good and it offends his dick. Can't stand it that a girl is better than he is."

I half-smile. Why is this bothering me so much?

Reid drops down to my level on his haunches. He says, "Look at me."

I do.

"Dude's a bigot, okay? First night we got here, he asked me where I was from. I said *Colorado* and he said *No dude, I mean where are you* from *from?* That's like the fifth time he's called me Mr. Miyagi. He's an *asshole.* He's weird about me being Japanese, he's weird about you being a girl, and he might be a good cook, but he's not as good as me and he's sure as hell not as good as you."

I kind of blink, momentarily distracted from my own issues. "He's said all that shit to you?"

"Like I said. Asshole."

"I should kick his ass."

Reid's mouth tips up. "God, I would pay money to see that."

"You didn't . . . you didn't need to like, step in and defend my honor."

"I know," he says. "I wanted to though. That okay?"

I think about it for a second. And say, "Yeah. Yeah, it's okay."

I don't know if *I'm* okay. I don't know because I'm not sure how to get "charity case," which I have heard about ten thousand times for ten thousand different reasons growing up, out of my head. But it's okay that Reid wanted to knock Andrew's teeth out.

It's okay that I think he might have backed up that threat.

Maybe it's because I'm very strongly considering doing the same thing.

"What do you need?" says Reid.

I say, "I'm good. I'm fine."

I stand up and brush myself off even though the floor in here isn't dirty.

And I climb up onto Reid's bed.

He's eyeing me like I'm full of crap, but he slides up there with me and lets me lay my head on his chest. Runs his fingers up and down my arm.

We turn on a cooking show, which is kind of ridiculous and obsessive, but hey, and I try not to let Andrew's words drown out the feeling of Reid's hands.

It's two a.m. when I wake up and text Reid. I haven't been able to sleep tonight. Playing and replaying the whole conversation and there's some kind of weird comfort knowing that Reid is probably up doing the same thing downstairs, for a different reason.

I reach over the side of my bed to brush my fingers over the care package that came in from my parents and Jillian today. It's nothing big—some candy, a little individual cherry cordial hot cocoa mix (my favorite), and a pair of aloe-infused polka dot fuzzy socks. I'm wearing the socks right now. I don't want candy in the middle of the night; I just wanted to feel the cardboard on my fingers. Tangible proof that I am known.

Touching the reminder that I am *believed in*.

I want to get my hands on a skillet or a pot or something and believe it, too. Prove to myself that I'm not here because I'm a girl.

It's a ridiculous thing to say, I know in my brain. When well over half of chefs are dudes, statistics would say that maybe *he's* here because *he's* a dude. But that doesn't matter a whole lot to my heart.

I've spent way too much time getting sneered at because I joined a club on scholarship or won something and got told it was because I was poor or *economically disadvantaged* or *in the right demographic*, and it's something I kind of want to talk to Riya about, because I'm sure she's gotten that crap WAY more than I have because she's Indian. Totally bullshit.

But she's asleep. And it seems inconsiderate to wake a girl up in the middle of the night to say, "Hi, can you please unearth some racial pain so I can feel a little better about my poor white girl problems? A boy said something mean."

Reid is awake, though.

And Reid will talk to me.

> **Carter:** meet me in the cafeteria.
>
> **Reid:** Yes ma'am.

He's standing there, even though we're not supposed to be in here after hours. It's just the tiny caf kitchen, so it's not a huge deal. But it's against the rules.

"Look at you, little rebel," he says.

"I'm not the one standing in the kitchen after hours."

"See what I get for trying to follow instructions for once."

I grin.

"So cross the line, princess. Equal opportunity incrimination."

I lock eyes with him and slide into the kitchen.

"I want to make drinks. You make two cups, I make two cups. And then I want to go outside. And try them."

He knows exactly what I'm doing. Trying to prove to myself in the smallest way possible that I have earned my spot. That I can win something.

He doesn't let on, though.

He leans over the kitchen island, weight on his forearms, and says, "You'll lose."

I say, "Indulge me."

He grins like he has fangs.

The game is on.

I can breathe.

The category, we decide, is hot beverages, because we are drinking these outside at three a.m. and that seems right.

It doesn't take either of us longer than ten minutes.

And then we're sneaking out the back door and disappearing over the hill and down the riverbank.

The river isn't running high right now. It's low and quiet, babbling more than rushing. Crickets are out and it's dead dark out here. I turn on my cellphone so we can see each other's faces.

"You are trouble," Reid says. His eyes are smiling.

"Don't stall. Drink."

Reid raises an eyebrow and the little insulated paper cup. He drinks at the same time I do. It is my best approximation of butterbeer, and it is *good*.

"Oh wow," he says. He downs the rest of it and my chest warms. From the drink in my throat, and the validation, and just watching him drink.

"My turn," he says.

We drink again.

His is this hot cranberry thing. It's sweet and spicy—ginger or something maybe? Could be some kind of chili; I can't pick it out—and dammit. His is better. We both know it's better.

We lock eyes and I say, "Moment of truth," and it is.

He looks at me, right into me, for a long moment. Then says, "Mine's better, freckles."

I blush. I've always been weirdly self-conscious about my freckles but it doesn't sound like a taunt coming from him; it's an endearment.

And I smile. That balloon expands back in my chest. Because he's right. His *is* better. And what that means is that he isn't lying to me when he says I'm good, when he says he thinks I'm as good as he is, when he says that he thinks I should be here.

He's telling me the truth now, and I hate that I need his validation, that I need anyone's, but that's where I'm at right now.

And what I do is slide my hand up into his hair and kiss him.

His hands are strong on my back and he pulls me up into his lap so my legs are around his waist. And it doesn't feel like this is a lie either.

It doesn't feel like a lie when I pull his shirt off or when he slides mine over my head. When I say, "You can touch me," into his mouth and he slides his fingers up under my bra, knuckles bumping past the underwire. When he kisses me so deep and slow I think maybe I'll die and my back is on the grass, river running beside us, and he scrapes his teeth down my neck.

It doesn't feel like a lie when I decide to touch him through his boxers and he says that's okay, too, and it doesn't feel overwhelmingly like this is going to end.

Even though it's going to.

I'm not suffocating on the nerves of it.

We don't go any farther than that. It's enough to kiss each other and touch each other in the dark by the river while everyone is sleeping.

I don't feel worthless, like Andrew laced into my brain.

I feel like I should be here, in this program.

I feel like I'm allowed to be *here*, on this grass with this boy. And maybe I'm lucky but maybe he is too.

I don't make it back to my dorm 'til five a.m.

I'm going to hate myself in an hour when Riya wakes up and I have no choice but to wake up with her.

But I don't care about the morning.

I care about now.

# CHAPTER TWENTY-THREE

When morning comes, I do, in fact, care about it.

But I don't regret staying out until a million o' clock. I am bleary and my eyes hurt, but I don't regret it. It's easy around Reid, shockingly easy, really. Judging comes and goes, and then there are six.

I kind of can't believe it.

There's Andrew, Addie, Will, Riya, Reid, and me.

The final six.

My total joy at somehow having made it here overshadows the little knife of annoyance that Andrew is here, too. The guy is a complete dick wagon but he can cook.

It's night and we're all hanging around by the fireplace, which I feel . . . almost possessive about. Like none of them are allowed to be here because this is where Reid and I go in the middle of the night. That is, of course, ridiculous. It's a *common room*. But I feel a little clench in my belly anyway when I come back from the kitchen with a glass of water.

I sink down on the loveseat next to Reid and he throws his arm around my shoulder without even looking at me, without taking a breath in this story he's telling. Like it's natural. Like we're A Thing. My mouth curls up and Riya catches my eye.

She smirks like *HA. I KNEW IT.* And I can't even say anything about it. She did know it.

I'm toast.

I shift a little closer to him so my hip presses against his, rib against rib. He says, "So yeah my mom reads 'the whole egg' on the box and thinks it means the literal whole entire egg and just tosses three whole eggs into the cake batter."

Addie says, "Shell and all?"

"Shell and all."

Riya is straight-up cackling. "White people, why."

Reid points at her with one hand and takes a drink from his bottle of root beer with the other, and says, "A question for the ages."

Now everyone's laughing, even Andrew, who looks a little grumpy at that last comment, but it's hard not to laugh at someone throwing actual egg shells into a cake.

"So she bakes the whole cake and gives it to her siblings and she has like ten million siblings, and everyone just eats it without saying anything. My grandpa is like, *I like these crunchies, what texture.*"

I'm laughing so hard I'm actually crouched over, afraid I'm going to spill my water and I think it's because of the story but also because Reid is here and I'm so freaking glad that I am, too.

"My dad, unsurprisingly, did most of the cooking."

"I don't know," says Addie, "I kind of want to try eggshell cake now."

"I'll go in halfsies with you on that," I say.

Will is being particularly quiet, I'm noticing, and I wonder if anyone else notices. Every time Riya laughs, his ears practically perk up. He's sitting at this carefully calculated distance from her, palm up, fingers relaxed and curled like he is *dying* for her to hold his hand.

I can't not see it.

Riya shoulder-bumps him and he laughs, then looks at the floor and sips his cream soda.

Addie is texting now, I don't know who. Maybe Cute Girl who got eliminated a couple weeks ago. There are definitely zero sparks between her and Andrew, thank the lord, because I would've had to have found some way to save her from herself.

But no. Addie would never.

Night gets darker, and everyone gets quieter, and I wonder if everyone is thinking what I am: that it feels like things are about to change.

The question hanging in the air: when are they going to split us back into individuals?

When does all this easy camaraderie split just a little further into fissures?

It feels like something coming to a close, and it makes me sad.

When it's midnight, late enough that I wonder if Reid will even be up at two, people start to head out. Tomorrow is our next challenge. No one wants to be sleepwalking through it.

Reid and I are the last ones to leave. I want to spend a minute outside with the fireflies, kind of clinging to the last few days in Savannah, so we stop at the bottom of the stairs. He needs to sleep, because apparently he is indeed going to be up in a couple of hours, whether or not he sleeps now. So he just leans in and kisses me right where my neck meets my shoulder.

And leaves.

I wait to actually shudder at how good it feels until he's turned his back.

Then I head outside. I'm going to miss the humidity, which Addie would possibly actually hit me over the head for saying, but there it is. I'm going to miss it.

And all the green, and the cicadas, even though they are kind of extremely annoying when they get loud, but they're peaceful. Almost meditative. Rhythmic.

I realize now, when tears actually start to fall down my face, how badly I want this. And acknowledging it feels like something.

It's terrifying. Wanting it this badly. Knowing that every single person back in that house wants it, too, and they're all *good*. Good enough to have gotten here, and good enough to still be here. There's a one-sixth chance I get it, and I wish . . . I wish I knew how much of a scholarship went to second place. Or third or fourth. Because there's a chance I get one of those and they're not enough.

There's a chance I fight for this so hard, and let myself want it so so bad, and then it just slips through my fingers and Savannah has already wiggled its way into my heart.

And it has.

It's there already, so deep that it would hurt like hell to extricate it.

Because the thing is, once you want one impossible thing, it's very hard not to want two or three or a thousand, and now I want all these big, impossible things at once.

I want this place for me. I want that scholarship. I want a place here that I am not fighting for every day.

Something breaks loose from my chest.

I *want*.

I stare up at the sky for a little while longer, listen to the cicadas and the wind in the trees, walk a few steps toward them. Breathe.

Then I turn back to go inside, and my eye catches on something.

Two people, the taller one pressed up against the damp brick of the school. The shorter one standing close. Now that I'm focused on it, I think they're whispering. My eyes adjust to the dark a little more.

It's Riya and Will, and she's against the wall. His hand is pressed over her shoulder and they're so close I bet they don't even have to make sound to hear what the other is saying. I'm staring like a creep, but I can't not.

There's a breath, and then Will's hand is sliding over her cheek and she's leaning into it. And he kisses her.

My heart flip flops; I've been dying for this. Because Riya has been dying for this, and because cocky, life of the party Will hasn't been able to stop staring at her from the second they showed up together. His hand tangles in her hair and hers slides down to one of his belt loops and they're just kissing—slow, languid, like they have all the time in the world.

He leans into her and she just sinks into him, and then I blink away. Because I think I am intruding on something intensely private.

It's not mine to see.

I practically prance inside and up the stairs.

And Andrew is still up. He's brooding.

"And then there were six," he says.

"Yeah."

I turn to head toward my room and he stops me just outside Reid's. "You know they're taking away the security blanket tomorrow, right?"

"What's that supposed to mean?"

"Means you won't be able to ride on your boyfriend's coattails anymore. It's just gonna be you. No way they head into picking the final four by pairs." He smiles. He's a freaking barracuda.

"Guess we'll see tomorrow," I say.

I turn and he presses his hand to the crook of my elbow. I jerk it away and think for a split-second about kicking Reid's door. Getting him out here to threaten to kick Andrew's ass again.

But then I look up at him, and I don't. I don't want to.

I don't need Reid to fix this for me, and I don't need anyone validating my right to be in this competition.

I puff up and say, "If you touch me again, I swear on everything holy I am gonna teach you firsthand the meaning of Rocky Mountain oysters. And there's no cows around for me to pull from."

He sneers. "I'm terrified."

"You think you're special," I say. And I just blow out a disbelieving breath through my nose, shake my head, and back away a pace.

"You just watch tomorrow," he says. "You and your little karate kid boyfriend—"

It is stupid.

But I am mad.

I reach out with *all* of my might, which, if we're going by muscle mass, isn't a whole lot, and I shove him.

I don't actually expect anything to happen. I am David facing Goliath; like the dude is huge and then there's tiny little lavender-haired, armed-with-naught-but-my-wits me, but he kind of teeters. He's off balance.

He falls. Right on his ass. Blinks up at me.

"I am so *sick* of your shit. This is not a *you can insult me but leave the people I care about of it* situation either. Stop insulting *me*. I'm done. I'm done with you. And as for the people I care about, keep Reid Yamada's name out of your fucking mouth. If you call him that shit or whatever the hell else you've been saying one more time, so help me."

He looks like a bull sitting there looking up.

"How about you just take your bigoted ass back to your room. And you just . . . you think about what you've done."

Am I trying to put him in time-out? Is that literally the phrase I just went for?

But here is what happens: Andrew stands up. Shoots me a dirty look. And he *leaves*.

He walks straight to his room and shuts the door. I wonder if he'll . . . if he'll spend some time thinking about what he's done.

I feel about a million miles tall when I walk back to my room.

And I sleep beautifully.

# CHAPTER TWENTY-FOUR

The kitchen is buzzing with energy.

Even Reid, unaffected, above everything Reid, is bouncing on his heels.

We're all waiting for the shoe to drop, because we all know. This is the day we get split up. We stand on our own merit.

The judges walk in a few minutes late and I bet it's on purpose. Maybe just because I'm looking for something to resent, searching for a place to direct my anxiety. But they walk slow, they sit slow, they smile slow.

Dr. Pearce stands and says, "The final six."

We all look at each other, just these nervous glances that are trying to bely confidence. Trying to posture, scare someone into making a mistake. I don't think I look particularly scary. No one really looks that scary.

Except, weirdly, Riya.

But it's because she's *not* trying to freak anyone out. She's the only one of us who is just standing there, hands in her pockets, blinking straight ahead at the judges. She looks relaxed. She looks like she is as comfortable in this kitchen as she is at home. She looks like she is calculating.

Here I am, shaking in my shoes over Riya; what a thing.

Dr. Pearce says, in that smooth English accent, "You should all be very proud of yourselves for making it this far. You are here because we have seen talent, promise, and technical excellence, in one way or another, from each of you. Of course, each of you is guaranteed admission to the school, as is everyone who has come through the program this summer. But scholarships are reserved for the top four. The amounts, apart from that of the winner, are to be determined. At this point in the competition, all teams are to be dissolved."

A little exhalation from everyone even though we all knew this was coming; it was a matter of time.

"The other change today is the matter of judging. Henceforth, there will be no elimination ceremony. After today's round in the kitchen, you will be evaluated, leave the room while we deliberate, and return to be judged immediately. One of you will be heading home today."

I swallow hard. I don't know why that's so much worse, but the stakes feel about eight hundred times higher, and no one's even started cooking yet, but I feel like every single oven and stovetop in this room is on.

I'm sweating; I think I'm sweating.

Dr. Pearce says, "You will have three and a half hours."

I glance over at Reid, and he looks down at me. Three and a half hours is like, astonishingly long for one of these things.

"You will all be making the same dish."

Ah, shit. This is never good.

"Beef Wellington."

*Shiiiiiiiiiit.*

Now even Riya looks nervous. Beef Wellington is cousin to baked Alaska on the impossible-to-master scale. If one of us had chosen it on our own, we could get points for ambition even if it wasn't perfect, but we all have to do it. Which means each piece of meat will be directly compared to everyone else's and shit shit shit.

"You are welcome, and expected, to choose your own side dishes, of course, but the Wellington is non-negotiable."

I tap my fingers at my sides. Fine, this is fine, this is fine. I can hold my own without help. And I *will*.

"Begin," he says with no fanfare.

Every one of us makes a rush for the meat locker, and we come back as a stampede armed with beef tenderloin. Riya is ambitious and going to make her own liver paté, because of course she is, and it looks like Reid may be going that way, too. I'm modifying the pre-made stuff because priorities. I don't know what Will or Andrew or Addie are doing but it doesn't matter. Looks like they're making Duxelles, which is a simple replacement. But I don't need to focus on anyone else. It's about the meat and the mushroom, and I'll be making my own puff pastry to blanket the thing, thank you very much.

I am determined to make it to the next round.

Especially after the whole Andrew incident last night. I can't go down before he does.

I think it, and then stop. No. This isn't about Andrew. It's not about him at *all*; he doesn't get to take this from me. Doesn't get to taint a single second of it.

I will move to round two for *me*.

Not as a screw-you to Andrew, not to Reid, for *me*.

I unwrap the tenderloin and throw some water in a pot to boil, then grab for the kosher salt and pepper. I sprinkle them both all over the beef. And wait. It's all about timing; it's *always* all about timing. Andrew is already starting his beef. Because Andrew understands the science of cooking but he is impatient.

Impatience never made an artist.

My water starts to boil and I throw all these little dried mushrooms into it. Some of them are sautéing the mushrooms fresh, but I like using the broth this makes.

I let my oven preheat.

And slowly, *slowly*, I start to relax.

I sear the edges of the beef in butter and fall into a rhythm. No one else is here in this kitchen. It's just me, and these ingredients, and these pots and pans and this butter, these shallots. It's a thousand things that have kept me company when the heat went out, when Mom and Dad were up talking too loud about how to pay rent when Dad's hours were cut at the store. Food and I feel like old friends.

I am not rushed mixing the paté and mushrooms, spreading it over the beef. Shingling this prosciutto and spreading the paté over it, then overlaying the beef with this *beautiful* masterpiece of meat. I season the whole thing a little and wrap it in plastic. Then let it rest in the fridge.

This is the trick to a perfect beef Wellington, among other things (namely, actual cooking skill): patience.

I wait.

The flavors seep into the meat while I putter around, grab a few fresh cut green beans, some almonds. Olive oil, sea salt. Sometimes complexity is what you want to go for, but beef Wellington is a million different flavors married into one, and it makes sense to me to pair it with something easy. Simple. Freaking delicious.

I won't need to roast them for a while, but they're ready.

Those, a pomegranate-based reduction to spread on the plate under the Wellington, and roasted crispy green beans and *man*, this is going to be good.

It's not even approaching plated and I'm already proud. Of what's in my head, at least.

I'm waiting for the clock to run down a little before I take the Wellington out; I want it to rest and marinate as long as possible before I make the puff pastry, cover the meat, and pop it in the oven. And I watch.

I watch Reid.

He moves through the kitchen with actual *grace*; I've never seen anything like it. It's like a ballet. He slides around the ovens and hot stoves with a skillet held up by his face, spins here and there to dodge open heat and moving bodies. Not a single burn. I would have scorched my skin eight hundred times moving at that speed.

He's just . . . good.

He sets his skillet down and glances over at me. Catches me watching.

His mouth tips up. He winks.

I look away, smiling, and wait a few minutes before I pull out what I need for the puff pastry.

It's relaxing, baking, even though I kind of hate it. Because it's methodical. Anything pastry-related falls into this category. So I can let the numbers do the work here and roll the pastry out and just turn off my brain.

Time starts to get a little sketchy, so I pull out the beef, wrap it in the pastry, toss it in the oven. The rest goes smoothly. Andrew is running around like a wild man at the last minute, plating, but no one else is, because we had a billion hours. If you're running at this point, honestly, what have you been doing since the challenge started?

The timer goes off. Hands off our plates. And every single one of them look amazing. Anxiety that has been beautifully suppressed up until now flares in my chest. Seriously, every. Single. Plate. Is perfect.

I grasp the edges of the counter as they go down the line. Riya's is cooked so beautifully I want to cry. It's that perfect balance between red and pink and the thing cuts like butter. The greens are perfect too, and of *course* so is the pastry; I swear it's like she's already been through a college chef program and back. Will's is more pink, less red than Riya's, and they question the sweetness of his side dish as a pairing, but it comes out cooked really well, and they're overall happy. Andrew's is too dry. As always. I grin. But they are *wildly* impressed with his roasted acorn squash, which is a damn work of art, the way it's laid out like flowers, the little sauce drizzled on it; it's gorgeous. And the meat has come out good enough. Then it's Reid. Freaking flawless as always, with these Brussels sprouts that he's flowered out so they look like crisp little roses. Addie, who has struggled with this meat: it's the lightest pink of all of ours, looks a little dry. The scalloped potatoes look like something I'd sell my birthright for, but the meat. She is wringing her hands.

And she should be, I think. Between her and Andrew, I don't know.

I am last. My throat closes up.

They slice into the meat.

And . . . it's *gorgeous*. Almost as beautiful as Riya's. A tad redder, tender, juicy, and they absolutely rave about the pairing of the meat with the pomegranate sauce. I think I'm supposed to maintain a professional expression, but I don't.

I can't not let this smile just spread across my entire face.

We are dismissed as they deliberate and the hall is quiet. No one is looking at each other, acknowledging each other, it's too much. The whole hall is filled with pressure, and I don't know how any of us can breathe.

It's only like five minutes before they call us back in but it feels like it's been an hour.

"Admirable effort," says Dr. Freeman. "This was a difficult dish and we were extremely impressed with all your offerings. Unfortunately, the most important part of this challenge was the meat. After deliberating, we are sorry to have to say good-bye to Addie."

Addie bites her lip. Her eyes go pink.

A stab of sadness needles through my chest.

"Th-thank you," she says. She gives us all hugs and heads out of the kitchen to pack.

I look over at Riya; we'll meet up with her as soon as we are dismissed.

Dr. Freeman says, "We will see you back in this kitchen the day after tomorrow." Then nods.

We leave.

I feel bad for Addie, but my heart is going a thousand miles an hour.

And then there were five.

# CHAPTER TWENTY-FIVE

Everyone keeps to themselves for the next day. Tomorrow hangs in the air—electric. Like that day before a storm, when the whole sky is just waiting. Waiting. Waiting.

Some of them, I have to imagine, are in the kitchens. I don't know where Reid is, don't know about Riya or Will or Andrew; apart from meals, I don't really know where anyone is or what they're doing. I know my room is empty.

And I know I absolutely cannot stand being in a kitchen right now. So I stay there by myself. I read. I try to force myself to think about anything but food, anything but tomorrow, anything but one of us going home and what if it's me what if it's me I can't afford this place without some kind of scholarship.

I lie back on the bed and call Em.

"She lives!"

"She does. She's going to die though."

There's a little swooshing sound, and I think Em is shifting around in her pillows. Getting comfortable. I wish I was there to have her pet my head and say, well, nothing to me because honestly, Em isn't really the comforting maternal type. But. I could count on the quiet head-petting.

"Why are you going to die?"

"Anxiety," I say.

"Tell me your woes."

"Tomorrow we get cut down to four. And I've been reading blogs; I think after that, it's just the one night's rest and then it's all four of you competing and they cut TWO. TWO, EM. And then it's the end. It's over and this is all over. And tomorrow? Whoever goes home tomorrow gets *nothing*. At least if you make it past tomorrow's round, you get something. I don't know how much; it could just be like a scholarship for books. Which, obviously that wouldn't work for me. But. Whatever it is, it's something. Tomorrow and you just . . . go home. Empty-handed."

"Really empty-handed though? I mean you still went and cooked and learned stuff and—"

"And the real scholarship was the friends we made along the way?"

I raise my eyebrow even though she can't see it over the phone.

She snorts. "Shut up, jerk."

I sigh. "I mean, yeah. Of course the experience will have been worth something. It's just . . .you and I both know that this place is *way* too expensive. Like pipe-dream expensive. I . . . ugh, I freaking need to make it past tomorrow, Em."

"You will," she says.

"How do you know?"

"I don't but what kind of asshole would say you're not gonna make it?"

"I hate/love you."

I can hear her smiling when she says, "I hate/love you, too."

It's quiet for a few seconds. Her doing who knows what, me just luxuriating in all this anxiety. And she just says, "Kick their asses tomorrow. Every one of them."

It is completely silent in the kitchens the next day. I mean, as silent as a kitchen can be. The air is filled with clanks and clangs and sizzling and that general chaos. But no one is flirting.

No one is smack-talking.

Not even Andrew. He's totally focused on the cooking for once, rather than on screwing me over or messing with Reid or any of the thousand things jackasses fill their time with. When judging comes, we are all basically vibrating with nerves.

I can barely think about the food because this, *this* is the round I absolutely have to get past. It's not likely, exactly, that if this was where it ended, I could justify going here. Even with whatever I'd get from making it to round four, I'd probably still have to stay home, do a couple years at community college, and then think about *possibly* paying for culinary school somewhere in-state. But still. Like. If I can just not go home today, there's at least a chance.

The judges move down the line, dish by beautiful dish. Meat-based again: swordfish.

Lemon-glazed and blackened and balsamic, and every way you could think to prepare it.

Everyone is sweating.

They make us leave.

We sweat more.

We come back from the deliberation waiting room and we all look like we've just jumped into a pool with our clothes on.

Dr. Kapoor starts speaking and my ears are actually ringing, I can't hear a thing he says. Except, "We are sorry, Andrew, but you'll need to pack your bags."

Andrew.

*Andrew*.

Not Carter.

I want to jump up into the air and squeal right here but that doesn't seem super sportsmanlike, so I stand there solemnly while Andrew stammers and thanks the judges and shoots me the dirtiest look he can conjure on his way out.

We are dismissed, and everyone waits an extra couple minutes so we don't have to run into Andrew crossing the quad.

Will is the first to speak. "Hell. Yes," he says. "*Hell yes*."

Riya smiles big and wide and Reid does this little Michael Jackson spin and I am just laughing because we made it. To the final round.

I almost can't breathe through the thought of it.

"Finals are . . . tomorrow?"

"Semi-finals in the morning," says Riya. "And then finals that night. Everyone stays though, I think, because scholarships don't get revealed until the end."

"Then home," I say.

Riya says, "Then home."

Last night, then. Is it really? God, that feels . . . surreal.

That feeling of total victory deflates and refills with anxiety because I can't stand the thought of it. Of leaving tomorrow and possibly never coming back.

I thought that the start of all this would be the most terrifying, the most pre-emptively painful. Just because no one knew what they were doing, none of us had any idea about *anything*, and there was that first week "What if I get sent home right now and have to tell my friends and family this was all a waste?" fear.

But this? This feels worse.

This feels like endless possibility caving in and curling around me and warping my muscles.

It feels like wanting and hoping and being terrified and what if what if what if.

Riya and Will walk on ahead and I don't even realize how slow I'm walking until I see how far ahead they get and how quickly it happens.

At some point, I guess I just stopped completely.

Reid laces his fingers through mine. He presses his mouth to my head and says into my hair, "You okay?"

"I'm okay. Just . . . just nervous."

"Me too."

I roll my eyes. "You aren't nervous like *I'm* nervous."

"Come on, Lane. Every one of us is about to chew our nails off. Look at me." I look at him. "I'm nervous."

He looks fine to me.

Unaffected, as always.

The sky is getting dimmer. Stars popping out. I am exhausted and electric all at once.

"Come hang out in my room?" says Reid.

My pocket buzzes. I feel shaky and nervous for a whole different reason now, for a hundred reasons, really. It's Riya saying, *Hanging out with Will for a while. Don't wait up.*

"Come see mine," I say.

Reid didn't look nervous before, even when he claimed it. But I can *see* it when he swallows too hard, see the little tremor in his hand when he brushes it over his hair. He's nervous now.

He says, "Okay."

# CHAPTER TWENTY-SIX

The walk up the stairs feels long; it feels charged. Like I have done more than ask him to hang out in my room, neutrally. Like friends do. Like friends platonically comfortably do; it's fine.

I'm maybe just picking up on him and feeding off it. He's so damn nervous I can see him planning out every tic of the smile he shoots me. *Curl up on one side, mouth. Then the other. A little higher; wait! Too high. You're being scary. Back to lopsided, do the lopsided grin.*

I laugh out loud and he just starts laughing, too, having no idea why I'm laughing and we are ridiculous.

We both stop for a second when we catch Andrew stalking through the hall.

He glares at us, like we sabotaged him.

Like it had nothing to do with him.

Then grumbles, "A one a.m. flight. Literally one a.m. On standby. What a damn waste—" Then walks off.

I am such an asshole for smiling, but Reid is grinning too and I know we are both imagining the satisfying justice of exhausted Andrew, waiting at one a.m. for this standby flight, furious in an airport.

We laugh at the same time when he's gone. And Reid cocks his head toward my door. He says, "On that note."

I push into my room and say, "Welcome to my humble abode."

"One of you is extremely messy."

"*You're* extremely messy." I close the door behind him and the little click almost makes me jump. I feel like I need to shake my hands out and do a couple pushups just to get rid of this sudden excess energy.

"So you, then." He laughs.

I curtsy. "Yes. Is that a problem?"

"No. I am extremely messy." He says it with a shrug and a smile that doesn't look mapped out.

I shove him in the shoulder and he wrinkles his nose in this adorably *Look at us, teasing. Innocently—god could we be more innocent and adorable* way.

Reid jumps back on my bed, shoulders stretched behind his head, all casual. Maybe it's a calculated casual—dude is a Slytherin, after all—but it's enough that I think I can calculate casual, too. So I jump up there with him. Like we don't have all night to ourselves. Like this isn't the last night before this ends, so it isn't basically a license to be impulsive.

I say, after *calculating* the exact amount that I should let my head shift over to his chest, and after he subsequently decides how much arm-over-my-shoulders to deploy, "What happens tomorrow?"

"I mean. A lot."

"Thank you, Captain Obvious."

"One of us beats the other, I guess."

I breathe out through my nose. "Not strictly true. We could both get knocked out in semi-finals."

"No. Power of positive thinking, Lane."

"Here is what I need to know. If I beat your ass tomorrow, are you gonna be pissed?"

Reid furrows his brow and shifts so he can look down at me. "You serious?"

I swallow. Well. Make a valiant attempt at swallowing. "Yes."

"You think I'm gonna be mad at you if you win? Honestly?"

"Well, I just—"

"You think I'm *that much* of an asshole?"

"No. I just. Listen, this entire thing has been built on a foundation of us hating each other and trying to beat each other and I just need to know. I need to hear you say it." I am firm, I am resolute, I am allowed to tell him what I need.

What I want.

I can want a thing, and stand firm on wanting it, even if it's unreasonable, dammit, and this is one of those things. I need to hear him say it.

Reid runs his tongue over his teeth behind his firmly closed lips. He looks at me and he's pissed. Such a shock, one of us being mad. Both of us being mad. But I don't care. I need to hear the thing. He doesn't protest, just sits with it for a second. Then says, "Carter. If you win tomorrow, I swear to god, I'll be happy for you. Okay? I'm not gonna be mad. I care about you, and even if I didn't, like, what. You think if Riya won, I'd be mad? Like I'm gonna cry if Will does? I want this as bad as anyone here but if you win, you win, and good. That settled or?"

I glance down at the bedspread. It was an unfair question probably because I knew the answer. But I'm not sorry I asked.

"And what if I beat you tomorrow?" Reid says. He wouldn't be asking it, I don't think, except I did. It feels like an afterthought.

I blow out a breath. "Then you beat me."

"Okay," he says.

"Okay."

And now I think we're both a little mad. Him at having his character totally questioned and me at him being mad, even though he kind of has the right, even though I kind of had the right.

"Maybe I should go?" he says. "It feels weird." I realize now that I've scooted away from him. "It feels like you want me to go."

"I don't," I say. I look up at him, scoot closer. "I swear I don't want you to go."

"You sure?"

"I just needed to hear it. I know you're not an asshole. Okay?"

Reid glances up at the ceiling and says, "I get it. No, I get it. It's a weird situation."

"Yeah," I say.

I slide my hand over an inch and then my finger is touching his.

"Last night here," he says.

Adrenaline is already rushing hard through me, from the fight or almost-fight or whatever, I think, but it runs harder and faster when his finger tightens on mine.

"It's weird. Knowing that," I say. "I'm like . . . surprised at how attached I am. To this place."

"Yeah, same." His fingers move so all of them curl around mine. "I'm really. Attached, too . . . to this—place."

I pull slowly back, dragging his hand with mine, so his fingers brush against the outside of my thigh.

"Let's just both win tomorrow. Split it 50/50," I say. His hand slips up to my waistband and waits there. For permission, I think.

"Fuck no," he says. He's smiling and this laugh cracks out of me. "If I kick your ass tomorrow, that scholarship is mine."

One of my hands is trailing up his shirt and I'm sliding over so he's practically on top of me.

"You're such an asshole."

He laughs. "You're baiting me, Lane. Like you'd give up a cent if you won and that scholarship was magically transferable."

He is on top of me now and I am *shaking* reaching for his jeans but I do it. "You're extremely right. I would have backed out on that deal the second it went my way."

"How dare you deceive me in such a way."

I say, "How dare I," and then he's kissing me.

Slow at first and then I'm like . . . I am overwhelmed with it. His fingers are skating at the hem of my jeans and I think he's dying to go for that button at the top because he keeps pausing by it but here is the thing. Right here— because I think we both have some idea as to where we want this to go—he's not smooth. He's kissing me like he's confident and a nervous wreck at the same time. And I don't know if he likes it when I touch his back, if that's

217

a thing or if he actually knows what he's doing, and honestly, I've done this twice, but I don't think I know what *I'm* doing, because if we do sleep together, well, it's not like if you've slept with one person you've slept with them all, and good lord, I am a ball of nerves.

My sex brain is rapidly overtaking my nerve brain, though.

I try to get the two to work in harmony.

Reid says, "Hey. Are you . . . how uh . . . Jesus. I don't know how to talk."

I raise my eyebrow.

"I am curious if . . ."

"Cat got your tongue, Yamada?"

He laughs this kind of throaty laugh, rests his head on my chest. "What I am asking is: Am I allowed to unbutton your pants?"

My heart jumps into my throat because actually *saying it out loud* is maybe one of the sexiest things I've ever heard? And I suddenly can't breathe over it?

"Shit, sorry," he says, and then I panic a little because I think he is interpreting my *Oh my god that's the hottest thing that has ever happened* as *Sir how dare you ask such a thing*. "We totally don't need to, okay? It's fine—"

"No, do. I mean. Yeah. Yeah, you can. I want you to."

I can feel his stomach expand against mine when he breathes and it's this moment of extreme relief and he unzips my jeans and I am feeling everything, like I swear I can feel individual atoms bumping against each other, and it is my turn to be presumptuous so I say, "Do you have a condom? I, uh. I don't. And maybe we're not gonna have sex here and I'm being total—"

"Shitttttttt," says Reid. "Shit. I didn't bring any because I've only ever done this with one other person and it did not even cross my mind—ugh."

"I didn't either." What a disappointment.

"Wait!" says Reid. "Hold up. There's a Rite Aid like right down the road. This is a college; people need these things all the time."

"Oh god."

"It's fine. Let me just . . . give me ten minutes?"

He gets off me and suddenly I'm embarrassed, like oh lord, him going to actually buy condoms means he is going to go do a thing that is an acknowledgment of what we are going to do. Oh lord oh lord. I say through my fingers, because my face is in my hands, "Okay, great."

"I'm the one asking the checker for this, short stack," he says.

"I know, just go. I am experiencing secondhand embarrassment for you and also something about buying condoms from Rite Aid is weird. Go buy the things."

Reid laughs and does this little adjustment maneuver that I am also embarrassed about, and it takes him eleven minutes from the time he walks out the door until he walks back in. And the thing about those eleven minutes is that they give me time to think past Sex Brain and it turns out, I still want to do it.

He comes back and my face isn't flushed and my heart isn't going 110 miles an hour but I know. In my head. I want to.

He sets the box on the bedside table and sits beside me.

"So are we doing this?"

"I mean," I say. "You bought the condoms already, so."

"So what?"

I say, "So we're kind of past the point of no return." I laugh.

"Okay, but that's not a thing that exists."

I roll my eyes.

"Carter." He shifts, so his feet aren't on the floor anymore, they're on the bed, and my legs are stretched out, but he sits with his knees bent up over mine. Takes my face in his hands. "We're not gonna do this unless you get that that is not a thing. Like I'm not just saying this? I'm telling you that just because I bought condoms, just because I spent money or something, doesn't mean you can't kick me out right the fuck now. I'll use them eventually." His mouth tips up and I smile. I'm blushing. "I don't care if we're like . . . having sex. You want to stop, we stop. I want to stop, we stop. Okay?"

Intellectually, I get that. I know that. It's just that sometimes it doesn't *feel* like that's a thing. It doesn't really feel like there's an e-brake you can pull without someone walking away mad or hurt or—

"Carter?" he says. "Just you and me here, okay? I'm not gonna be pissed at you if you don't want to."

"Okay."

"And anyone who would is an *asshole* and fuck them. Well. *Don't* fuck them. Whatever."

I laugh and say, "Okay. I get it. No, I get it. Do you want to stop?"

When Reid laughs, it's downright hoarse. "Extremely no."

"I don't either."

"Okay," he says.

I flick the lamp off and pull off Reid's shirt and he kisses me, slides me back until he's on top of me and I'm on the pillow, unbuttons my jeans and slips his hand over my underwear. Both of us are in our underwear now and what he's doing doesn't feel totally smooth, doesn't feel rehearsed or calculated, but it feels *good*, like so good I think I might actually come apart.

I shimmy out of my underwear and so does he, and then we're in nothing and I'm a little glad the lights are off and a little annoyed at them at the same time.

In the time it takes me to unclasp my bra—every teenage boy thinks that is a thing they'll be good at and every teenage boy is wrong—Reid has gotten a condom out of its wrapper and slipped it on.

I suddenly feel like I should say something, like I need to fill the air with something that isn't just the crinkle of foil and this quiet waiting. "How are we going to get back to hating each other now?" I say.

Reid laughs. Breathy. Kind of quiet. Says, "It's gonna be a challenge but I think we're up for it."

"If anyone can . . ." I say.

Reid does this kind of dorky two-fingered salute of acknowledgment. Shifts up as close to me as he can get. Whispers, lips brushing my ear, "You good, princess?"

I say, "Yeah. Are—are you?"

One more hoarse laugh. "Yeah. Yeah I'm good."

There's a flash of nervousness on his face and then it's gone and neither of us really has the room for nerves because this is happening. It's happening and both of us have been dying for this, and it's *good*. It's so freaking good and I'm so happy and I don't regret it for a second.

221

I don't regret the wanting.

Because when you finally *get* what you've let yourself be desperate for, it makes the terror of wanting so. So. Worth it.

# CHAPTER TWENTY-SEVEN

So Reid never actually left my room because we both passed out, and Riya did, in fact, come back some time in the middle of the night, which means that this morning opens up with a *lot* of embarrassed laughter from, like, everyone, and at least all of us are dying together.

Reid looks sheepish for the first time since I've met him, possibly for the first time in his *life*, when he waves at Riya, coughs, and says, "Well. I'll, uh, see you guys at breakfast. I just have to. Leave the room with no excuse."

Riya whistles at me when he leaves and I say, "Like you have room to talk."

She smirks.

I hop in the shower, and when I get out, Riya says, "Competition in thirty minutes. We should head down."

I say, "Yeah, good call," but then stop. My gaze snags on her bags, all zipped up, puffing out because for some reason it's impossible to pack nearly as efficiently when you're going home as when you're going somewhere new.

Something twists in my chest. It's the last day. The *last day*. I don't know how to deal with how unreasonably sad I am about it so I don't.

I go downstairs with Riya, waiting to pack until I absolutely have to, and we all sit at the same table. We'll be cutthroat rivals in twenty minutes, but right now we aren't. We are four kids who want to have breakfast. Want to enjoy this last little piece of time until it all changes.

Reid keeps smirking at me and shoulder-bumping me all through breakfast and my face heats up, blood quickens. I'm a blushing mess all through the meal and I'd be embarrassed about it except Riya and Will keep flirting so freaking hard that I don't think either of them notices that either of *us* is even breathing, let alone blushing.

Reid says, "How you doing?"

"About . . . last night? Or about fifteen minutes from now?"

He shrugs, mouth tips up. "About any of it. All of it. How are you like as a unit?"

"I'm extremely good about last night."

Reid scrapes his teeth over his lip and smiles, goes for another bite of cereal.

"About fifteen minutes from now," I say, "I don't . . . I don't know. I'm. Some sort of adjective."

"Ah. Informative."

"I am nothing if not forthcoming. How are *you*?"

"Good and an adjective. A different one than you so you know I'm not copying."

I roll my eyes and smirk, and Reid elbows me gently, tips his head toward the cafeteria door that leads out in to the quad.

"You ready to go do this thing?"

"Nope."

"Gonna go do it anyway?"

I look at him, suck in a breath. "Yep."

"Let's go."

It takes about ten seconds to realize something is off about the kitchen. I don't know what, I can't pinpoint it. But something seems just ever-so-slightly wrong.

Nerves rush over my skin. I can *feel* the anxiety pooling everywhere and I'm sure it's drowning every one of us.

I zero in on Dr. Freeman when she speaks. "Welcome to the penultimate challenge. Two of you will move forward after this round. You have three ingredients in front of you. Duck, cooking wine, and blood orange."

I raise my eyebrows. That is bizarrely easy.

I glance over at Reid and his brow is furrowed.

Duck, orange, and wine? That's literally the perfect combination. It would be like . . . like setting peanut butter, jelly, and bread in front of someone and saying, "GOOD LUCK MAKING SOMETHING OUT OF THIS. BWAHAHA."

Now I'm even *more* nervous. Somehow. Apparently that was possible.

"You have a half hour," says Dr. Freeman, in that smooth voice that sounds like wine personified. "Begin."

I shrug. Don't look a gift hors 'd'oeuvres in the mouth.

I start coming up with a marinade, incorporating the wine and the blood orange, which is *gorgeous*. Some garlic. Pepper. The spices are fresh and not picked over, which is a nice change of pace. I hadn't realized how nice until this moment. But I can breathe when the kitchen isn't totally cluttered, a stampede of cheffery. I'm still nervous but letting the rhythm of this take over me, only letting myself think about what I'm doing, what I'm cooking, I can't think about Reid or Will or Riya or the judges. It is me and this couscous and this duck. The end.

I pull a pan out from an open cabinet and that's when I realize exactly what felt so off when I walked in here: so much of everything is missing. Not the ingredients. But the pots, the pans, the spatulas, the spoons.

*What the hell.*

I frown and set the pan on the burner, melt a little butter in it. All the butter slowly slides to one side.

That's . . . extremely weird.

Gotta be a faulty pan. I pull up another and see without setting it on the stovetop that it's got a big bubble right in the middle of it. Then it dawns on me: It's all like this. All they left us is damaged cookware. Partially burned up, torn up spoons, only plastic cheap spatulas that can't withstand heat like a metal one would, pans that are warped and uneven and that have lost their non-stick coating.

I should be scared.

I should be panicking.

But I'm not.

I'm *thrilled.*

I'm not the only one who grew up without money; Riya doesn't have any either. I know Reid at least isn't rich. I don't think he's . . . like me. But he doesn't live in a mansion. The only one I don't know about is Will.

So. I don't know if it's a *huge* advantage that I've spent my whole life cooking on decade-old cookware, that everything I've ever made in a skillet has been a battle between me and whatever is in the pan, and its particular wicked quirks that force the ingredients to go all over the place in unpredictable swirls and burn patterns. But it's not a disadvantage.

I weigh the original pan in my hands and watch the butter. See exactly how fast it moves, pick out the bumps. And I go for it. The duck sizzles and oh my lord it is *heavenly*.

One by one, a chorus of swear words from the boys in the room rises up, and I'm just smirking. This duck is coming out perfect.

It's *perfect* and I am manipulating the pan with my wrist and the couscous is flawless and the sauce tastes like a dream and I want to cry.

I want to cry because I am going to *make it*. I am going to do this, I am going to do this, oh my god, I am going to do this.

We plate.

Everything smells like the most incredible thing on the planet, whatever that is, and terror combined.

I am shaking so hard I think I'll drop my plates.

I don't.

The buzzer rings; time is up.

The judges go down the line, sampling everything, and I am so freaking frozen with anticipation that I don't even hear what they say about *my* dish. I hear nothing at all. I feel every hair on my body stand up and feel the blood rushing through my veins and I feel the *thoughts* spreading through my brain.

Good lord, am I going to have a stroke?

Maybe this is what it feels like. A heart attack. Something.

We head into the deliberation room, and Reid sits next to me, squeezes my hand so hard I think my knuckles will crack. His palms are sweaty. Maybe those are mine. My leg is bouncing so hard the table is shaking but no one cares and no one talks.

The air feels solid.

Dr. Lavell comes to get us, and we file back into the room. Everyone is just . . . breathing. We are all stiff and looking at the floor and breathing.

Or trying to.

Dr. Kapoor clears his throat. "Congratulations, competitors, on making it this far. And on providing us with easily one of the most challenging semi-final rounds we have had the opportunity to judge."

Breathe, breathe, breathe, breathe.

It's fine, you're fine, your lungs are not collapsing, you are okay, this is fine, whatever happens. WHATEVER. HAPPENS.

Dr. Kapoor says, "Proceeding to the finals: Riya Khatri."

I blow out a breath. Reid is squeezing my hand again. I am dying.

It's not a surprise; of course Riya made it.

"And the final competitor moving to the final round—"

My heart is in my throat. I am become sweat. I am become death.

"—is—"

Lord, just strike me with a bolt of lightning right here right now.

"Carter Lane."

I burst into tears.

# CHAPTER TWENTY-SEVEN

I can't believe it.

I can't *believe* it and yet, here it is. We are dismissed immediately and everyone looks dazed. For totally different reasons, we are all just blinking, eyes glazed, staring at the ground. We have two hours until the final round and that feels so soon, and it feels a million miles away, and I don't know how to handle it.

I know I have to pack.

I know I have to head to my room. One foot in front of the other.

No one talks, really, we just walk in a group back to the dorms, but Riya breaks off with Will—she has already packed; no reason to hang out in our room all afternoon—and Reid breaks off with me.

We walk up the stairs together and everything feels small. I'm thinking that I am so proud of myself I can't stand it. And I'm thinking about Reid and how he must be devastated and then I feel a little guilty but I shouldn't feel guilty because I earned this. I did. I earned it.

Then we get to my room and I sit on the bed, surveying the mess on the floor and everywhere, and try to plan an attack on all my clothes. Reid shuts the door behind him and now my thoughts have shifted somewhere different. I am thinking about him and me in this bed last night and waking up next to him and a hundred feelings I don't know how to name, and all these thoughts are just tumbling and tangling together in my head.

I look back at Reid and his face splits in a smile as he leans against that door.

"Congratulations." He's still smiling and it's genuine. His voice cracks a little, but he means it. He's proud of me, I think, and he's just leaning there looking all handsome, arms folded, against the door. And I slide off the bed to slip my arms around him. This is probably one of my top ten moments. Maybe top five. Three? I don't know how to quantify it. All I know is that I feel like sunlight personified. I got this. I did this. All on my own.

Reid's arms fold around me and he rests his chin on my head. He smells like the kitchen—like butter and spice—and I breathe him in. His breaths are even when he whispers into my hair, "You earned this, princess."

I blush from my head to my toes.

But something sticks. Something, a barb just right there snagging on my chest.

There it is: that little buzz of doubt.

I say, without letting that doubt take root, "Are you okay?"

"I'm fine," he says.

That cracked hoarseness in his voice. Like he's so sad but doesn't want me to know.

Besides that, he's okay. Steady and even and solid and smiling like he's supposed to. Congratulating me. For taking this thing he wanted so badly from him.

231

Like he expected it.

I press my nose into his chest and say, "Tell me one thing?"

He says, "Anything."

"You—you didn't let me win. Did you?"

The hand that's been running up and down my back freezes. "What?"

I regret it almost instantly but it's out there now. "You didn't let me win." I know as I say it that he didn't, of course he didn't, that I *am* good enough. Maybe better than him. Better enough to be heading into finals.

He slides out from the door, chest brushing my face. Holds me at arm's length.

He says, "You think—you think I would do that?"

I blow out a breath and keep my eyes trained on the door for a second.

"No," he says. "Of course I didn't."

I say, "Okay."

We're both quiet for a minute and under my skin is buzzing this current of *Are you sure? Are you sure? Are you sure?*

And I guess one of them makes it out of my skin and pops out through my mouth.

Because Reid says, "Am I sure? Am I sure."

I sigh.

"Look at me," he says. "Look at my face and tell me I *let you win*. That I didn't want this so fucking bad I could taste it, Carter."

I look at him. His eyes are red-rimmed. Wet. He is one step away from crying.

"I lost!" he says. "Okay? You win, you're better than me, congratulations. I lost because you're *better* and it's fine, it's freaking fine."

"Whoa," I say. "Little resentful, are we?"

Reid blinks.

I immediately want to apologize.

I don't, though, because I halfway think I'm right.

He says, voice low and measured, "Don't put that shit on me."

His voice is hard now; Reid has gone from sad to mad in a heartbeat. Here we are again. This is so damn familiar. So. Damn. Familiar.

"What do you mean, *don't put that shit on me*?" I say. "You're mad."

"I'm not mad that you won, Carter. I'm mad that I'm the one who should be sad here and here you are, asking me to comfort *you*."

"Reid, come on."

"You're asking me to fucking reassure you. Maybe I'm the one who should be being *reassured* right now? Jesus."

"What, I need to reassure your ego? Do I need to apologize?"

"No, you don't need to apologize—"

"This is such bullshit," I say, and I am so mad. I'm so mad I'm shaking. Reid looks exhausted. I don't care. "I have to feel guilty. Once again. For asking a question. All you had to do was answer it, but you're like . . . lashing out at me instead. You're pissed. Admit it. You're pissed that I won."

"I'm not pissed you won."

"Yes, you are."

His nostrils flare and he glances away from me, and that's how I know he's lying. "Carter."

"YOU ARE. ADMIT IT."

"OKAY," he says. "I'm pissed. I'm pissed! I wanted this so bad and you got it and I wasn't gonna say anything because I know it's bullshit, but damn! I'm not allowed to feel *emotions* over this?"

"You're supposed to be happy for me!"

"I am happy for you," he says.

"You're mad. You're disappointed."

He laughs and it's not funny. "Humans can have more than one feeling at once, Lane."

"The sarcasm is helping."

He looks up at the ceiling and shakes his head.

"I asked you *one question*," I say.

He says, "You asked me if I cheated to let you win. You asked me if I'd cheapen everything for both of us by doing something so bullshit. That's not a simple question."

"I don't believe this."

"That makes two of us."

I am vibrating. I can't stand him and I can't stand this and I can't stand having the best day of my life tainted by Reid's selfishness.

"I should go," he says. He's reaching for the doorknob at his back.

I say, "Look at us. Finally agreeing on something."

Reid curls his lower lip over his teeth, runs his tongue over it. He yanks the door open.

"I'll see you in finals," he says. And he slams the door behind him.

I'm so mad, I'm throwing all my clothes into my bags, as though this is my clothing's fault.

How dare he. How *dare* he ruin this? I'm regretting everything, all of it, because he's being so immature and I should be allowed to enjoy this and I can't.

This is my last day here. What bullshit.

I wish I hadn't kissed him and I wish I hadn't touched him and slept with him and fallen for him. What have I been thinking? What have I been *doing*? This selfish boy . . . and I wrapped my heart in butcher's twine and handed it to him like a gift.

This boy who had done nothing more since the moment I met him than try to get me to fall.

Everything hurts. I am a wonder of contradictions. I am thrilled and furious and happy and sad and how how how does a person even begin to contain all these emotions at once without just exploding out of their skin?

I need to think about finals. About cooking. About what comes next, and not about Reid and how stupid I was to think this had a prayer of working.

I breathe in through my nose, out through my mouth. In through my nose, out through my mouth.

And when I'm done packing, I leave my room and head downstairs. I want to walk outside alone, to the river. It's sweltering outside; I can breathe in all the hot humidity and it tastes like everything I want so badly. It tastes like my heart yearning and breaking all at once.

Everything is electric and everything hurts.

I walk toward that river, the one we had that picnic by? The river that feels like it's calling me to stay here. To earn this.

God, I want it so bad.

I move toward it, needing a moment of peace, and stop short.

I see him and he doesn't see me. Reid. Sitting under this tree. He's clutching a paper, the letter I assume has to be his acceptance to this program, in one hand. His shoulders are shaking and he's tipping his head back, leaning it against the rough bark of the tree trunk.

And he's crying.

Tears and red eyes and sadness and I know it then. I know it then like I knew it all along. Of course he wanted this. Of course it is destroying him that he didn't get it. Of course he didn't give me the victory.

It stabs into my chest all at once, a flurry of arrows.

I'm not going to comfort him. I can't.

I'm still furious and I bet he's still furious and this is private.

This is not for me.

I walk away.

And let him cry.

# CHAPTER TWENTY-NINE

The kitchen feels like a battleground.

I mean, I guess it could be what with all the knives and fire, but I don't plan on murdering Riya, and as far as I know she doesn't plan on murdering me. I allow my mouth to curl up when I look at her, standing on the other side of the kitchen, fingers tapping on the counter.

She smiles back at me, and I'm glad it's her. Of everyone.

I shut my eyes. Exhale.

Will is here, at a chair beside the judge's table. There's an empty chair next to him, which hurts my heart. I feel guilty but I also feel mad, because how immature. Just not to come.

It's fine. I don't need him here.

That is painful to think because he's been a constant in my brain in the kitchen since day one, and somewhere along the line, that all shifted from hating him to . . .well.

But I'm standing here on my own, and it's true. I earned this. This is mine and it's not his and I do not need him in this kitchen in order to function.

Dr. Pearce says, "Competitors. You will be given ten ingredients."

*Ten. Damn.*

"You may choose to use them in whatever way you please, in however many courses you feel you can complete in ninety minutes. Every ingredient must be used. Is that understood?"

"Yes, sir," we both say, just slightly off-rhythm of each other.

We get our baskets and there is a host of things here. Some odd, some totally commonplace. Peppers, shrimp, chocolate milk powder, some kind of big stalked vegetable thing I think is called a cardoon. Both of us will absolutely use the first ten minutes at least just planning.

Dr. Pearce smiles big and bright and says, "Begin."

I stare at the ingredients and begin separating them. A soup, where I can use the cardoon, braised, probably the shrimp. A beef main course where I'm going to use the chocolate because dessert is too easy for that. The peppers can go in the dessert. Radishes in the beef. And it goes on like that until I think, I *think* I have something worth serving. By the time I make my decision, Riya is already firing up the oven and the stovetop, setting bowls and spoons on the table. Thankfully by now we have good cookware.

I start with the soup base, let it boil and the flavors seep in through everything, really get *character* in the liquid. Then I marinate the meat and start grinding peppercorns. I lose myself in it. Let it melt into me, this thing that I love more than anything. I'm completely overtaken in spice and the taste of everything savory on the air, in the steam that rises from the pot, in the smell of brown butter in that pan—so overtaken, in fact, that I almost don't notice when Reid walks in.

He shoots everyone at the judge's table an apologetic look and ducks in front of them to sit beside Will. And when he does, my eyes have left him about eight hundred times because I am focusing on this food. But he locks eyes with me.

Does this almost-smile that lights me up.

It's uncertain, shaky, a question mark. But it's a peace.

I take a breath of a moment to consider it, and then I go back to this.

To what I came here for.

The clock ticks down in a wash of broth and Parmesan crust and spatulas and sizzling pans. Until the time comes to plate. We are used to this by now. There is none of that beginning-of-the-summer last-minute dash to desperately plate, no question as to whether we'll make it on time. Of course we both will. We are smooth and composed and each have everything done a full sixty seconds before the time runs out. Mine looks good. The soup is beautiful and golden brown, the meat is perfect, that chocolate intermixed with Panko and about a thousand other ingredients. The soufflé with the raspberry and pepper is a work of art.

So does Riya's, though. It's more pastry, baking, scientific, like she said she loved to begin with. There's this breathtakingly beautiful salad with giant croutons she clearly baked herself. A main course of portobello mushroom and shrimp over this rice thing that looks so good I want to crawl over the counter and eat it all right now with a spoon. Cake, at the end. I can't decide the flavor but everything, *everything* looks incredible. From both of us. We look like we can compete.

For the first time in maybe ever, I am absolutely certain I deserve to be here.

We both do.

I look straight ahead while the judges taste, offering little commentary.

And I wait it out alone when they dismiss us. Everyone does, I think.

It is in the dead heat of the day when they finally call us to the amphitheater. Just like they used to.

We all sit in the front row—me next to Riya, Riya next to Will, Will next to Reid. Will and Riya are holding hands and my heart jerks but it's fine. It's fine it's fine.

Dr. Lavell stands on the stage with the rest of the judges and tells us she's so proud to have worked with all of us, she wishes us the best of luck on our futures, she hopes to see every one of us at the Savannah Institute of the Culinary Arts next year. It's all a blur. I'm praying for it to speed by so I know the end, and slow down so I can savor this with a clarity of memory, all at once.

She says, "In fourth place, with a half tuition scholarship, Will Malik."

Will stands, smiles wide, and approaches the stage. He shakes hands with Dr. Lavell while we clap. Accepts his award.

We know the next award will go to Reid and he takes his time walking up those stairs, confident as hell like always, accepts the three-quarters tuition scholarship with a smile and looks directly at me. I don't smile, but

I don't look away from his eyes. I clap as hard as anyone. God, this hurts.

Then, the moment of truth. They announce that the second-place winner will receive a full tuition waiver. That these awards thus far are higher amounts than they've ever given, but that this year, the competition was outstanding, and they've been given an allowance. First place gets everything. Room, board, books, everything. But full tuition would maybe be possible. I think maybe . . .

I grab Riya's hand and her knuckles whiten around mine.

"Second place goes to . . ."

Every organ in my body has squeezed up into my throat.

"Carter Lane."

The breath leaves my chest. Riya starts crying.

I walk up those steps, proud and thrilled and . . . I take the award. Sit.

A little sad.

But Riya's eyes are bright and she's laughing so hard when she accepts that award and I just love her and I think I knew, I think we *all* knew that Riya deserved to win. That she is better than every one of us.

I glance over at Reid, but he's not looking at me.

He's smiling and clapping for Riya.

That's okay. That's good.

I wish he had his arm around me. I wish I could be so happy but be comforted right now.

I understand, suddenly, how you can be happy for someone and sad for you all at once.

# CHAPTER THIRTY

No one has much time to hang around after judging is over. We have time to grab our bags and get to the airport. We're all in one bus, which is nice, but it's crowded, and that only matters because I don't . . . I don't get to talk to Reid.

I *want* to talk to Reid, basically need to talk to him, but it doesn't really matter. Because I can't. I can't say what I need to say in front of all these people. And I don't know what I need to say, really. I definitely can't fumble through it.

Maybe I shouldn't.

I don't know.

I'm so tired, in this adrenaline comedown, and everything is sinking in. I didn't win and Pell Grant won't cover everything I need, but I can take out some loans. I can go. To Savannah. I'm going to. I'm *going to*.

That's a dream, it's incredible.

We all go through security together. Shoes off, bags laid out, all scanned. We part ways at the gates, and I hug Riya so hard she chokes. She swears she'll request me as a roommate next year and I swear it back and she and Will go.

Reid's hand jumps to the back of his neck and he opens his mouth to say something.

Then he stops. Looks away. Says, "Have a safe flight."

I say, "Yeah. You too."

And that's it. The end of it.

Not like it really had a prayer of working out in the first place. Not like relationships that start out with as much raw hate as we had wind up these amazing forever things that change your life.

Now that everything is setting in and roommate promises are being made and I've called my best friend and my parents and my sister, the thrill is giving way to the loss. Because it was infuriating and he was infuriating and I'm sure I was, too, but it was . . . something. And I think maybe I had started to love him.

And I can be excited.

And hurt.

All at once.

The next hour and a half goes by slow. The clock ticks down and time feels like viscous liquid. Nothing like it felt in the kitchens, like there was never enough. I'm having a hard time not rushing through everything now, actually.

Just sitting.

Not anticipating.

I'm so tired now. I could just nap right here.

Boarding begins.

I wait until all rows get to board because I'm of course in the cheapest category, then I stand and get in line.

And I think maybe I'm in a movie, because I hear, "Hey, Purple Haze."

I freeze. I don't turn around because it's not him, there's no way it's him. It's the first thing he ever called me, but it can't be him. This is over.

Again, his voice. A little closer. "Pumpkin."

A smile jabs at my mouth and I am reluctant to let it take over.

Very close. "Princess."

I inhale. Exhale. Inhale. Exhale. Force my heart to beat.

I turn around. "You lost?" I say.

"Nah." He shakes his head.

"I wondered if you'd be in the air already," I say.

"Not yet."

"Go back to your gate, Reid."

He smirks. Says, "This is my gate."

"Prove it," I say and I reach for his boarding pass. He snatches it back out of my reach—tall jerk—and smiles.

"What are you doing?" I say.

"I need to talk to you."

"Well you picked a lousy time to do it. We're boarding."

Reid says, "So get out of line and wait 'til the end. Or stay and ignore me and I'll just stand here, giving this speech to no one."

I look at him, his eyes so dark and earnest, and my heart is beating out of control and of course. Of course I get out of line.

Every cell in my body wants to apologize, but I don't. Maybe I will later but not yet.

Reid can breach that line. If he wants.

There's a foot of space between us but his voice is low, like there is no one else in this crowded airport. Like the sounds of takeoffs and landings and crying babies and stressed adults yelling into cell phones don't exist here.

He says, "I'm in love with you, Lane."

And that is not what I expected to hear. My mouth drops open.

"I'm sorry about being an asshole. Back there. It's just . . . you get it? You get that it's hard to untangle shit? I'm glad you won. I'm glad you beat me if you deserved it and you obviously did. Okay? I shouldn't have been a jerk about it, not then."

I look at the ground. My hand finds my bicep and I run my fingers over the skin to ground myself. "I should have just . . . been confident on my own. Not basically forced you to choke out that you lost. I was an asshole, too."

"Well," he says.

I look up at him. "I saw you crying. Out there by the river."

He looks up at the ceiling, "Oh, awesome."

"I was a jerk."

"We're both jerks. That's kind of the way this works."

I grin, in spite of it all.

"I love you, Lane," he says again. "Like I tried to just sit still in this airport and wait to board like everyone else, pass the time sucking down a shitty coffee and reading some celebrity gossip magazine someone had left lying around, but I couldn't even focus on a heavily photo-graphed article about Harry Styles because you wouldn't get out of my head. Do you understand the kind of hard-core feelings it takes to distract me from Harry Styles?"

I laugh. Hard. Just in surprise, I guess. "You love me? You sure about that? I've made your life hell all summer."

"That's how I prefer it," he says. "I bet you love me. If you really thought about it."

"You must be the cockiest boy alive."

He shrugs. "Who has a magazine? I could give you the Harry Styles test."

The line moves forward.

"You're exhausting."

He says, "Yes."

"And infuriating."

"Obviously."

"I wish we had more time to do this."

He says, "I don't. When I ask you, in a few seconds, if you love me, and you say no, I can just walk back to my gate and by the time I get there, you'll be in the air. It's the perfect strategy."

"And what if I say I do?"

Reid swallows hard. "Guess I'll reconfigure."

It's quiet.

The line shrinks.

"You love me?" he says.

He's . . . nervous. I can see it. He's not really that cocky; he's so freaking anxious he can't stand still.

And I don't think about it. I just say, "Yeah. I do."

Reid smiles, teeth on his bottom lip. "If this was a movie, I'd say, *Then don't go. Stay with me* or something, but I'm going to Colorado."

"That's not that far from Montana."

"Hop, skip, and a jump."

"And a year isn't that far away."

"Nah."

I say, "Are you gonna go? To this school?"

"Of course I am," he says. "If nothing else, I'll get several opportunities next year to kick your ass, princes—"

I grab him by the shirt and kiss him. He only needs a heartbeat to recover and then we're kissing like today never happened, like we never split up, like mileage between us doesn't mean a thing. His hand curls around my neck, in my hair. The other slides down my back.

I feel everything in every cell of my body.

And we don't break apart until the ticketing agent clears her throat. It's just me left.

Reid says, "I'll see you."

I say, "Yeah, you will."

And I go. I don't turn back.

I board the plane, and I already have a text waiting.

> **Reid:** So tomorrow night. Pencil me in for like a FaceTime competition. You and me and cooking with NO UTENSILS.

I smile so hard my face might actually break.

> **Carter:** You're on, Yamada.
>
> **Reid:** Yamada. Always with the sass.

I put away my phone.

Take in all the safety info.

The plane hurtles down the runway, its wheels lift, and it hits the air.

I fly.

# ACKNOWLEDGMENTS

In my experience, a book, without other people, is a jumble of words that never gets shaped into a story. This one was no exception.

Thank you first, to you, dear reader. To anyone reading these words, anyone who has blogged or said anything on social media or said words to friends or who picked this book off a tangible or digital shelf anywhere at all, THANK YOU. You are why I get to do this.

I also want to shout things out to my crit partners, who had a significant hand in the making of this book. AS ALWAYS, you are my favorites. Sara Taylor Woods, actual soul twin—thanks for so consistently being such a moderating influence. Rae Chang, loveliest sharpest foodie, someday we will band forces to craft the greatest meal the world has ever seen. Tabitha Martin, greatest cupcaker of all time, thank you for being an utterly magical human.

To my agent, Steven Salpeter, for believing in me and my work so enthusiastically (and always having excellent tea advice). To my editor, Nicole Frail, thank you so much for making this writerly dream of mine real.

To all of you in my little corner of the writing community, you are always helpful in a million ways, and make this solitary profession so much richer.

Lastly, to my amazing husband, and my boys, for not only tolerating but loving late nights and hurried dinners and tangents and rambling imagination and all the things that come with being my people. (And being my people when I'm on a deadline.)

To anyone I may have forgotten, to anyone reading this, again, thank you.